Messed With The
Wrong One

TANISHA STEWART

D1526230

Messed With The Wrong One: An Urban Romance Thriller
Copyright © 2021 Tanisha Stewart

Books may be purchased in quantity and for special sales by contacting the publisher, Tanisha Stewart, at tanishastewart.author@gmail.com.

Cover Design: Iesha Bree
Editing: indieink.net

First Edition
Published in the United States of America
by Tanisha Stewart

Table of Contents

Dear Reader,

I hope you enjoy this urban romance thriller. Once you finish the story, I would love it if you left a review. Not sure what to say? It's fine – just comment on the characters, or your overall thoughts on the book.

Pressed for time? You can also just leave a star rating (1 = low; 5 = high). Either way, I would love to hear from you. I read all reviews left for my books and often use the feedback to improve future releases.

Lastly, if you would like to connect with me, feel free to join my reader's group, Tanisha Stewart Readers, on Facebook, or my email list at www.tanishastewartauthor.com/contact.

I look forward to hearing your thoughts and interacting with you!

Tanisha Stewart

Synopsis

We all do things we live to regret, but when you mess with the wrong ones, you get what you get.

Junior cheated. Marlena is furious. She resolves to teach him a lesson. What starts as a simple act of revenge, however, quickly takes a dangerous turn. While Marlena is busy getting back at Junior, someone else happens to be planning a revenge of her own against Marlena. The deadly kind.

Marlena finds herself in a race against time to no longer change her man. Now, she has to save him. And herself.

A Quick note: This story was inspired by a "Freestyle Friday" challenge created by Ebony "EyeCU" Evans, founder of the EyeCU Reading & Chatting group on Facebook.

Ebony inspires authors to sharpen their skills and show their creativity. Her challenges have inspired me greatly, leading to four separate releases, including this one with its cast of crazy characters.

Sit back, relax, and enjoy.

Messed With The
Wrong One

Chapter 1

Marlena spun the block, completely pissed that she had to go through this again.

"I swear I told this nigga... I swear. I told him." She wiped her eyes for the third time since she started driving.

Junior thought he was slick, sneaking out at three o'clock in the morning like she wouldn't feel him getting up and pretending to go to the bathroom. She'd gone through this one too many times.

But now it was...

She shook her head with force.

"This fucking GPS!" she screamed.

Marlena was so mad she punched her dashboard. All it did was hurt her knuckles.

She winced from the pain of hitting it at just the wrong angle but tried to breathe deeply to soothe the pain.

"We gotta find him, Mar..." she told herself. "We gotta find him."

Marlena knew what Junior didn't.

He thought he was being slick, and she thought she was being slicker, but you reap what you sow. Sometimes before you even sow it.

The GPS rerouted for the fourth time. If Marlena wasn't so bad with directions, she would have been at her friend Shaniqua's house fifteen minutes ago.

"How the hell did Corey know about Shaniqua, anyway...?"

The color drained from Marlena's face as she realized how. There were only one of two ways. Either her cousin, Corey, had had an encounter with Shaniqua himself, or he knew someone else who had.

Either way, if she didn't get to Junior fast enough, he would have more than just the shame of being tricked into sleeping with another man on his hands.

Junior would have HIV.

***

Corey started second-guessing himself. *Maybe I told Marlena too much,* he thought. His favorite cousin was always good at putting two and two together.

No time to dwell on that now, however. He had to move forward with the rest of the plan.

***

Marlena finally pulled up to the address she'd navigated to from her screenshots. She felt breathless as she exited her vehicle, despite the fact that she had driven here rather than ran.

Maybe it was the fact that she'd spoken to herself in a heated fashion the entire way over. That was a quirk of hers. She could hold entire conversations all by herself, asking and answering questions, and hosting full multi-sided debates. She wasn't crazy, though. That was just how she processed things.

She noticed Junior's car was still there and almost turned around and went back home. It infuriated her that she was out here trying to save his ass, but he had fallen so easily into her trap after promising her he would never do her wrong again.

"Fiancé, my ass!" she huffed.

Junior couldn't keep it in his pants if I paid him, apparently. He'd just proposed a week ago.

Disgusted, Marlena spat on the ground as she considered whether Junior was even worth it. If he'd already had sex with Shaniqua, Junior was a dead man.

Well, that was cold, Marlena's mind told her. Of course, there was a chance he'd used a condom. Not that he had before with that other bitch, who he'd gotten pregnant...

Marlena shook her head to clear those thoughts. That wasn't what she was here for.

"I guess since we're here, we're doing this," she muttered, then made her way to the front door, preparing to bang on it like she was the police.

When her fist raised, however, she was stopped mid-movement by something attached to the door. It was a Polaroid photo and a note stuck just above the knob by clear tape. Marlena ripped them both off with one swipe, taking some of the paint off the door in the process.

The note was scrawled in ugly handwriting, but it was easy to read, nonetheless. *Catch us if you can, BITCH!* it read. The photo was of Junior lying on the ground, bound, gagged, and seemingly unconscious, while Shaniqua posed next to him, one hand on her hip, an evil smirk on her face, weave cascading down her back and over her shoulder, and her other hand throwing up the peace sign like she was chucking Marlena the deuces.

"Us? Who is us?" Marlena asked. Her head whipped to the left, and she noticed Junior's car was the only one that was parked in the driveway.

Shaniqua had apparently kidnapped her man. Marlena had to find out why.

Chapter 2

Junior woke up in a pitch dark, closed environment. His hands and feet were bound with rope like he was in a cowboy movie or something. *What the hell is this?* he thought.

The last thing he remembered was that he was going to meet up with his friend, Shaniqua. She'd said she needed help fixing her laptop because she didn't have enough money to have it done by a professional. Since Shaniqua made it seem urgent and Junior couldn't sleep anyway, he decided to go over to her house at three o'clock in the morning.

Now that he thought about it fully, that was a dumb ass move. Look where he was. Junior's memory was still fuzzy, but he definitely remembered seeing Shaniqua's face, her opening the front door, him walking in, and then everything going black.

What the hell happened?

He didn't have long to try to figure it out because the trunk door opened, and his assailants were revealed. Shaniqua was smiling evilly down at him, and she was standing next to...

"Reggie?" Junior blinked to refocus. He couldn't be lying in a cramped-up trunk on account of his best friend.

His mind swam.

"Reggie, what the hell, man?"

Reggie shot him a smirk that mirrored Shaniqua's level of evil.

"Surprise surprise," he said, then reached his strong arm down to aggressively pull Junior from the trunk, letting him fall to the floor like dead weight.

"Fucking pussy!" Reggie shouted before kicking Junior in his ribs.

***

Corey drove through the dark highway, mentally rehearsing what he would say when he met up with his girlfriend, Regina.

His cousin, Marlena, was more like a sister to him than a cousin. He couldn't believe he'd betrayed her in this way.

She definitely deserved it for what she did to Regina, but... this was OD.

He had to tell Regina that he was out. He'd gone along with her plan because it made sense to him at the time, but now that Marlena was probably running around like a chicken with her head cut off, Corey felt guilty as hell. She had blown up his phone multiple times since he sent her that stupid ass text about her boyfriend Junior, and he, going along with Regina's plan, had ignored all of her calls. "This is not what we do, bruh," he said to himself. Corey and Marlena were thick as thieves. "Why didn't I just..." he started, then remembered why he hadn't just come out and told Marlena that Junior was cheating. It was because that would do nothing to help Regina, his love.

Corey shook his head. This situation was complicated as hell. Maybe relationships just weren't for him. After his last breakup, he didn't give himself a lot of time to heal. Maybe his emotions were too raw, and that's why he wasn't thinking straight.

He reached toward his phone on his dash to call Regina, but overthought it again. He didn't want her to break up with him. If he wanted to show Regina he was down with her as her man, he had to prove it.

Was hurting his cousin the way to prove himself to his girl though? Or was there another way?

***

Marlena's mind was going crazy. She needed to figure out what was really going on with Junior and Shaniqua, and why. What problem could Shaniqua possibly have with her?

Marlena's mind flashed to the police station as she was passing it, but she decided against getting them involved. Even though she had solid proof her man was kidnapped, she felt in her heart this was something she needed to handle herself.

Maybe it was the fact that it was four o'clock in the morning now, or maybe it was the fact that she just might be a little crazy, but Marlena was determined to find out what gave Shaniqua the inkling that she should have the fucking audacity.

"Must not know about me," Marlena mused, then felt deflated at the thought that all this had blindsided her.

She pulled back up to the apartment she shared with Junior, ready to develop a plan of action.

When she got there, she saw yet another note and picture taped to her door with the same kind of adhesive from Shaniqua's place.

"These niggas had time today," she said to herself. She examined the note and the picture of her old high school. Marlena graduated ten years ago. Why was Shaniqua having her meet her there?

"Girl, you are getting way too ahead of yourself," Marlena said. Here she was thinking her high school was somewhat connected just because the picture was of her alma mater. This note was written in the same handwriting as the other. *And so the plot thickens,* was what it said.

Marlena snorted. "Whoever is doing this has way too much time on their hands. What, are they following me?"

But she knew she had to go. Her mind was intrigued, despite her frustration mixed with fear for Junior's safety.

Chapter 3

After Reggie beat the hell out of Junior for a good five minutes, he was finally ready to talk. "Think you can take MY BITCH, nigga?" Junior had no idea why Reggie only screamed some of his words when he was mad. He always did that, ever since they were kids.

At the same time, he still had no clue as to what Reggie was implying.

"What bitch, Reggie? Come on, man. Untie me. I gotta piss like a motherfucker and my arms and legs are killing me."

Reggie wasn't budging.

"Come on, man!" Junior pleaded again. "For real! I never stole no bitch from you. You and I go way back. You already know this."

"Oh YEAH, muthafucka?" Reggie said. "What about Marlena?"

Junior froze. There was no way Reggie could have figured that out.

Reggie nodded with a chuckle. "Yeah, nigga. I know. You thought you was real smooth with that catfish shit, but I figured it out."

Junior still tried to play it off. "What are you talking about?"

"I went through Marlena's phone. Briella, nigga? Really?" Briella was Reggie's little sister's name. Reggie only saw his younger sister on occasion since Reggie's

9

mom had given full custody of her daughter to Briella's father. Junior used Briella's name to catfish Marlena through a messaging app. He pretended to be a messy female who was giving Marlena the tea on Reggie when Marlena and Reggie first started dating three years ago.

Marlena and Reggie had only been dating a month at the time, but Junior felt that he had way more chemistry with Marlena than Reggie did, even though he was the one who actually hooked the couple up.

Marlena bit the bait, accepting the innocent photo of Reggie with his arm around one of their neighborhood friends, Regina's, shoulders as the two laughed at a joke.

Marlena had broken up with Reggie that day, refusing to listen to his excuses.

Junior approached Reggie a couple of weeks later after hooking him up with another chick to take his mind off of Marlena.

Reggie was so into the other girl that he didn't take any offense to Junior stepping to him about his *former fling,* as he called it.

Reggie and the other girl ended up breaking things off with each other a year later, well into Junior and Marlena's relationship.

"What do you mean you went through Marlena's phone?" Junior asked, still playing dumb. "That doesn't make sense, Reg."

He knew that was Reggie's sensitive spot. Reggie had always been a little *touched,* as the older ladies would say it. Any time someone insinuated that he was crazy or stupid, Reggie would try his best to prove them wrong.

Unfortunately for Junior, Reggie wasn't falling for it this time. "Like I said, I went through her phone that night after we all watched movies together." Reggie was cool, calm, and collected as he spoke. "She left it accidentally, so I had it the whole night. I looked through all her messages, and to my surprise, she still had some on her messaging app from a girl named Briella. I can't believe you used my sister's name for that bullshit, and that fake ass Instagram model's picture."

Junior was about to open his mouth to deny it again, but Reggie continued.

"Yeah, muthafucka, you thought you was slick. How else would some random chick get a picture of me and Regina? Knowing good and damn well me and Regina wasn't messing around." Reggie's eyes grew dark for a second before they changed back. "Thought you was slick," he repeated himself. "Then you jumped on my bitch almost immediately after we broke up. I peeped game at the time but I didn't have no proof. Now I got it nigga. You fucked with the wrong one."

Junior knew he was caught red handed. *Shit!* he thought. Apparently, Reggie had never gotten over Marlena, which was why he went through her phone. That was weird in and of itself, since Reggie and Marlena only dated a month, but apparently, Reggie had developed much deeper feelings for Marlena during that time than he had let on to Junior. Being deeply in love with Marlena himself after years of dating, Junior could see why, but he couldn't take back the hands of time. He had to figure out a way to appease Reggie, and quick. Reggie was bound to do anything to him. Junior knew his best friend already had at least one body under his belt. Reggie had told him so, but Junior promised to never speak on it.

"Reggie, please untie me. I gotta take a piss, for real."

"PISS YOURSELF, BITCH! Then burn in hell...." Reggie giggled, then pulled the .45 revolver from the back of his waistband, pointing it down at Junior's face.

Chapter 4

Marlena pulled up to her old high school, looking around the parking lot to see if anyone was there before getting out of her vehicle.

It was a Saturday, and she only saw one other car in the vast expanse of empty spaces. She walked toward the front steps of the school, and as she got closer, she saw a small, black object laying on the third step.

It was a cell phone on top of yet another note. Marlena sucked her teeth. "At least they didn't use that damn tape this time."

Press 1, then the green button, the note said.

Marlena rolled her eyes. Shaniqua and whoever she was working with were getting on her last nerve. They really thought they were doing something, sending her on a wild goose chase like this.

She just prayed Junior was okay, but part of her didn't even want to save him anymore.

The screenshots Shaniqua had sent of her conversations with Junior were clear evidence that he was cheating, yet again. Or, at least, he was going to before they kidnapped him.

"Should just let them keep his ass," she breathed, but another part of her heart went out to him. When Junior wasn't cheating, he was the best man she could ask for. He was everything she prayed for, and more. He was sweet, charming, attentive... the list went on and on. He just could not for the life of him stop flirting with other women, and he seemed to have a real problem with infidelity.

Granted, he'd only cheated once, but once was enough for Marlena. She'd actually dated Junior's best friend, Reggie, briefly before she started talking to Junior, but her chemistry with Junior was always stronger.

She and Reggie's relationship didn't work out, ironically, due to him cheating, but she and Junior had hit it off.

Three semi-blissful years later, and here they were.

Marlena was so confused.

"Should I call this number, or leave it alone?"

***

Regina sat impatiently waiting for her boyfriend, Corey, to arrive. She hoped his silly ass hadn't gone and told Marlena what was really going on. She'd hate to have to be the one to...

Corey was sweet, but he was too sweet. That was always his problem, along with being too trusting. It was easy as hell to flip him on his flesh-and-blood cousin, all over a cock and bull story Regina told him about Marlena getting her fired when they worked together.

No... Regina's beef with Marlena was much deeper than that, and Shaniqua and Corey were the perfect people to help her get that bitch back.

***

Shaniqua pushed Reggie's arm to stop him from shooting Junior. "Chill, calm down," she said.

14

Reggie gave her a look like he wasn't planning to shoot Junior at that moment, anyway.

They both watched as piss seeped from Junior's jeans to the ground underneath him.

"Nasty ass..." Reggie said with a devilish smirk, then put his gun in the front of his waistband. He looked Shaniqua up and down, licking his lips. "Come on. Let's go talk in the back."

Shaniqua blushed but followed. Reggie was fine as hell, and she had been waiting on this opportunity. He didn't need to know her little secret.

When they got to the back room, however, all of a sudden, she felt nervous. Reggie did have a gun. What if he suspected something? What if he figured it out? They were already planning to get rid of Junior. Shaniqua was sure Reggie would have no problem getting rid of her, too, if he deemed it necessary.

No, she told herself. *It's too risky. Plenty of other fish in the sea.*

Shaniqua needed a distraction to throw Reggie off from the true reason for her change of plans. His strong, muscular arms reached toward her, but Shaniqua held back, forcing her face to remain neutral so she wouldn't betray her emotions.

The way Reggie was glistening under the soft light, coupled with his broad chest and the sweat trickling down his back that she could see through his wifebeater, Shaniqua was tempted to just go for it, but she needed to keep her focus.

"You know what? It's probably not a good idea to leave Junior alone in there," she said. "You can get out of a rope pretty easily."

Thankfully, Reggie wasn't the brightest bulb in the box, so he didn't question her. He walked back into the main room of the abandoned building where Junior was still laying, and Shaniqua followed.

Chapter 5

Regina looked out the window, yet again, waiting for Corey to arrive so they could go ahead and be done with this plan.

She pulled out her phone to call him and tell him to hurry up, but before she could press his name in her contacts a message came through from Shaniqua. *Meet me at this address,* it said.

Regina contemplated for a second whether she should call Corey to tell him to go there with her but decided against it. He was already getting soft, she could sense it. She couldn't let him know everything. She had to go leave the notes for Marlena on her own. He also knew nothing about the plan to kidnap Junior... or Regina's other recent activities. Regina shrugged. "Whatever," she said.

She was about to be done with Corey, anyway. She grabbed her keys and left the apartment.

***

Shaniqua quickly put her phone away before Reggie could see her texting Regina. He was busy with his back toward her, walking over to Junior. Something wasn't right about all this, she could tell. Maybe Regina could help her find a way out.

***

Marlena sat in her car, mentally stuck. She was still holding that stupid cell phone in her hands along with the note. Part of her wanted to call the number as the note instructed, but another part was ready to just let Junior go and start fresh. She felt bad for him getting kidnapped, but that was what he got for cheating. Or trying to, at least, if he didn't go through with sleeping with Shaniqua.

Another part of her didn't like how brand-new Shaniqua was acting. What the hell made her switch up like that? There had to be more to the story, but it didn't make sense. Why would Shaniqua flirt with Junior all that time, get him to finally agree to come over, then kidnap him?

The wheels started turning in Marlena's mind. There was definitely more to this story, and she was going to figure it out.

She turned the key in her ignition to start up her car.

***

Junior was pissed to see Reggie and Shaniqua back so soon. He had already slid his blade from his back pocket without them noticing. His plan was to free himself while they were having sex, then bust the hell up out of this random ass abandoned building.

Now, he had to move much more slowly and subtly. If they saw his arms moving, they would figure him out.

It was extremely difficult, and not to mention, uncomfortable to try to cut the thick rope that had his arms tied behind his back. Also, his ankles had all but lost circulation due to being tied together so long, but

Junior was in a fight for his life. He had no idea what Reggie was capable of.

Well, actually, he did, and that was worse.

He looked up at Shaniqua, hoping for a distraction. "How do you even know Reggie?" he asked.

Reggie stepped around her, bent down, and sneered in Junior's face. "Shut the hell up, piss boy! This is MY woman." He pointed at his chest as he spoke. "Soon as we kill you, I'm taking her out of the country."

"Kill?" Junior said at the same time that Shaniqua said, "Out of the country?"

Reggie rose back to a standing position and smiled at Shaniqua. "Yeah, babe. I think we would make a good couple." His eyes darkened as he turned back to Junior. "I think I'll be over Marlena once I'm through with her, too."

Junior's heart dropped at the mention of Marlena. Reggie was planning on killing her, too? Why? Marlena was the innocent one in all of this. She had nothing to do with Junior's actions. He opened his mouth to tell Reggie so, but Shaniqua cut him off.

"Reggie, you didn't tell me anything about us going out of the country, baby..." Her voice was nervous as she spoke.

"Oh, come on, ma. Don't bitch up now. You been riding for me so long."

Riding for him so long? Junior thought. He tried to put two and two together. Shaniqua was his friend, not Reggie's. To his knowledge, Reggie and Shaniqua didn't even know each other existed. Clearly, that was wrong, seeing that they kidnapped him together, but what was their connection? He decided to ask since they were planning to kill him, anyway.

Maybe it would help him to develop a plan.

Maybe it would buy him more time to save Marlena.

He looked at Shaniqua yet again, trying to play on her softness. "Niqua, why are you doing this? I thought we were friends. How did you and Reggie even come to know each other?"

Reggie looked down at Junior again. He cracked a grin. "That's a good ass question. Bet Junior never would have believed I could pull something like this off." He nudged Shaniqua. "Tell him, girl. Tell him how we met."

Chapter 6

Three months prior...

Shaniqua's story started way before she ever met Reggie, Junior, or anyone else in this fucked up situation. Her story started when she was a child.

Shaniqua always felt like she was different from other boys. Her birth name was Shawn, but she had always believed she was born in the wrong body. Even when she tried to tell her mother and father, they didn't want to listen to her, until one day, her mother caught her with her pants down, trying to cut her penis off with some scissors.

"Shawn!" her mother screamed, rushing over. "What are you doing?"

Shaniqua was already bleeding and also crying. It stung so bad, but she wanted it gone. Her mother wrenched the scissors from her small fingers, throwing them across the room, then grabbed a hand towel to wrap her son's tiny member.

"You might need stitches," her mother said, avoiding the deeper issue. When Shaniqua fell silent, her mother, Shaundra, finally delved into what was really going on.

"Why did you do this, baby?" she asked in a gentle tone.

"I told you I wasn't a boy!" Shaniqua cried.

Her mother was silent until they were in the car on the way to the hospital.

While she was driving, Shaniqua's mother started asking questions about Shaniqua's feelings. Shaniqua told her that she always felt she was really a girl, and not a boy like her parents told her. "I want my name to be Shaniqua," she said. "And I don't want to dress like this anymore."

Shaniqua's mother made the decision that giving in to her child's wishes was better than watching her suffer.

Shaniqua's father, on the other hand, wasn't having it. When he saw Shaniqua and her mother come into the house with shopping bags full of clothes, shoes, and accessories, he was heated. It was like he sensed what was happening, despite the fact that Shaniqua's mother hadn't told him yet.

"Where the hell were y'all?" he asked.

Shaniqua's mother just looked at him. "We were at the hospital, baby. Shani... let me talk to you in private." She brought the clothes to Shaniqua's room, turned on her TV, and told her to stay there while she talked to her father. Shaniqua obeyed, but soon, she heard her parents yelling.

She'd already felt uncomfortable with herself before this, but that was the first moment her discomfort turned to hatred.

***

As time wore on, Shaniqua's parents' arguments continued to grow deeper. Shaniqua's father refused to call her anything other than Shawn. He kept calling her *his son*, which made Shaniqua hold resentment toward him, on top of the hatred she had for herself.

When Shaniqua's mother changed Shaniqua's birth certificate without his permission, that was the straw which broke the camel's back. Shaniqua's father filed for divorce. Her mother was heartbroken, and Shaniqua's hatred for herself and her father grew stronger. She began to cut herself in secret. She found that hurting herself in this way would sometimes help to ease the emotional pain.

Her mother never dated again after that, and she ended up dying from breast cancer five years later.

Shaniqua was fifteen at the time, and none of her family members wanted her because of her identity, so she became a ward of the state.

She refused to let her mind remember those times. She pushed them far away, deep into the crevices where even she could not penetrate.

Then one day, she decided she'd had enough.

Men always seemed to have a problem with her, starting from her father. Her father never bullied her outside of refusing to call her by her preferred name or pronouns, but boys at school and her foster homes did everything to her that her father didn't.

When she turned twenty-one, she underwent the process to transform her outward appearance.

By the time she turned twenty-five, she was ready to get even.

Chapter 7

Shaniqua already had encounters with three other victims before she met Reggie and became entangled in his twisted scheme. With each of the men she victimized, she followed the same process: befriend them on social media, message back and forth with all kinds of flirty pictures and emoji's, meet up with them and have sex, then send them a picture of her original birth certificate and a childhood photo, mixed into a collage with a photo of the two of them in bed together.

Shaniqua would demand a fee to keep quiet about what happened, then be on to the next. It was a nice little side hustle, and she'd already gotten six thousand dollars from those three victims.

She was in the middle of flirting with her fourth, when Reggie approached her three months ago.

She hadn't realized what his real goal was at the time. Shaniqua thought he was genuinely interested in her. Reggie approached her while she was exiting a nail salon that was next to the barbershop he frequented.

"Hey, sexy lady," he said, giving her an irresistible grin that caused her heart to palpitate. In her twenty-five years of life, Shaniqua never had a crush develop this strongly or quickly. It was like she was swept away by Reggie with those three little words he uttered. She knew immediately that wherever this man went, she would follow. Whatever he wanted, she would deliver.

"Hey," she said, trying to keep a straight face. She smoothed a hair behind her ear.

"What you about to get into today? I'm Reggie." He extended his hand, and Shaniqua shook it. His hands were so strong, so smooth. Shaniqua imagined being wrapped up in his muscular arms, and those strong hands gripping and caressing her all over.

"Shoot, nothing. I'm Shaniqua. What are you about to do?" Shaniqua decided at that moment that even if it was just a one-night stand, she was down. She needed Reggie in her life, bad.

Reggie pulled out his cell phone. "How about you give me your number? We can link up later tonight."

Shaniqua eagerly divulged her seven digits. She even added the area code, though her number was local. Reggie smirked, probably picking up on her desperation easily.

Shaniqua had no idea what Reggie's true plans were at that moment, but she did now.

***

Regina lived in the same neighborhood as Reggie and Junior for all her childhood years, up until they went to high school. They grew up with each other. Even their moms were friends.

When Regina moved away, she was sad to leave the neighborhood, but her mom wanted to have her spend her high school years in a better environment.

High school was where Regina first met Marlena. Well, met wasn't exactly the best word. She encountered Marlena, was more like it.

Marlena was one of those pretty and popular girls, while Regina was considered a loser. She didn't have the latest styled uniforms like the other girls. She didn't have the cute headbands and socks and sneakers to wear to make her outfits pop. Regina's mother was poor, so all of Regina's clothes and shoes came from secondhand stores. One of her uniforms even had another girl's name etched on it, something she was teased about endlessly.

Then, the worst happened. Regina's mother was laid off from her job only a month into Regina's academic journey at her private school. She could no longer afford the tuition, so Regina was sent to a public school, a different one from the school Junior and Reggie went to. She met girls like Marlena at her new school, too. They were just as snobby and just as bitchy.

Regina dealt with all of their bullshit until she graduated.

As an adult, she no longer let anyone fuck with her without getting dealt with.

One way, or another.

Chapter 8

Shaniqua was nervous as all get out when she was preparing for her date with Reggie. She agonized over just the right dress, the sexiest heels, the perfect shade of makeup...the list went on.

Finally, she found a look she felt would work for her and made her way to the restaurant. It was a Red Lobster, which was ironically one of her favorite places to eat. She was mentally rehearsing the entire way there how she would come out to Reggie. She hoped he would still accept her. The unshakeable chemistry she felt caused her to pray over and over that he would.

Unfortunately, there was no need for those prayers. That became evident about five minutes after she sat down. Reggie was pleasant, but it became very clear that he considered this a business meeting rather than a date.

"Listen, lil mama... I got a proposition for you," he began.

Shaniqua was confused at first. When they'd met earlier that day, Reggie had sort of flirted with her. Was he doing that again now? It didn't feel that way. His words now felt kind of cold and distant, and his smile didn't quite reach his eyes. Also, for the first time, now that he was up close and personal, she could see the darkness in his pupils. Shaniqua had never met a person with black eyes, but Reggie fit the bill.

She shuddered.

"You cold?" he asked, offering his jacket.

Before she noticed how scary Reggie was, Shaniqua would have gladly accepted his jacket. At that moment, however, she shook her head. "No, it was just a chill. What's up? What kind of proposition are you talking about?"

Shaniqua swallowed back her emotions as Reggie perked up. It was clear from his body language that he never saw her that way. Romantically. This was true with every guy she'd had a crush on, but she thought this time things would be different.

Still, she listened as Reggie explained. "I got this nigga that needs a lesson taught to him. I think you're the woman for the job." He winked.

Woman for the job? Did Reggie know who she really was? How? Her victims had bought her silence, and she never breathed a word of their encounters to a soul. How could he know? Did one of them tell? Suddenly, Shaniqua felt uneasy, like this situation was not going to end well for her.

"What kind of lesson?" she asked, keeping a poker face as she swallowed her emotions again.

Reggie sighed. "Listen, you're a beautiful woman. That's the only reason I'm asking this of you. I promise you will be paid handsomely." He reached into his pocket and pulled out a stack of money. His pants were baggy, so Shaniqua hadn't noticed the bulge. Her eyes widened.

"That's six thousand dollars." He slid the money across the table to her, and she had enough experience from her brief stint working at a bank before she got fired for stealing money to see that these bills were real. Still, she thumbed through them, feeling their freshness and inhaling their scent.

"What do you want me to do to this guy?" she asked. Now she felt uneasy again.

Reggie smirked at her nervousness. "Relax. It's nothing crazy. Let me tell you the plan."

***

Regina felt like she just could not win in life. After graduating high school, she opted out of college. She was done with school. She couldn't stand any of the people at any of the places she went, and she couldn't think of a single subject that she wanted to spend another four years learning about.

She briefly tried getting a cosmetology license, but she ended up dropping out two weeks into the program because the bitches there were catty, too. Regina didn't know if she gave off a vibe or what, but it seemed like everywhere she turned, she met girls like Marlena.

She didn't know why her mind was so focused on Marlena, though, until one day she looked in the mirror and figured it out. They sort of looked alike. Remove the blemishes, add a little makeup, and voila! Regina could pass for Marlena any day, but she felt she would never have Marlena's life.

The boys flocked to Marlena in high school. Regina saw as much during her brief period of attending the same institution as her. She imagined the girl was married off by now to some millionaire or something. She certainly seemed to be going places.

Regina ended up working at a factory job, and to her great surprise, both Junior and Reggie, her old friends from her neighborhood, were there! They worked the same section as her. When they saw each other, both Reggie and Junior gave her a hug with no hesitation. It felt like old times, except both of these brothers were looking brand new to Regina.

Reggie had filled out tremendously with his solid, muscular build.

Junior was the lankier of the two, but that didn't take away from his obvious six pack abs, and he had Reggie in the height department.

Both of them were blessed with full, sexy lips, and thick, well-groomed beards. Junior sported fresh waves that fit well with his caramel-colored skin tone, while Reggie was of a darker hue and sported starter locs.

Regina swooned internally at the sight of these men. What she would give for a piece of either of them. Or hell, both at the same time. She wouldn't even care if they spread her business.

The trio picked up their friendship like they'd never lost touch. They ate lunch together every day, chilled together and everything. Both Junior and Reggie were single at the time, too, so Regina felt like all she had to do was take her pick.

She wrote in her diary incessantly, trying to figure out which one she liked more.

Regina finally decided on Reggie, then Marlena reared her ugly ass fucking head.

Chapter 9

When Marlena started dating Reggie directly after Regina selected him as the man she wanted to make a move on, Regina was furious.

How dare she? Regina was just starting to get over her comparisons of herself with the bitch, and now she was stealing her man right from under her before she had a chance to stake her claim. And what the hell was wrong with Reggie? Why hadn't he mentioned that he met someone? It seemed like one day he just popped up with a girlfriend without telling Regina anything.

When Reggie finally revealed the news, Regina couldn't help but give Junior the side eye, too. She wondered if he had known about Reggie and this bitch, Marlena? Junior could have given a warning or something.

Regina silently stewed for weeks, then she decided if she couldn't have Reggie, she would have Junior.

One day, they came by her new neighborhood to see her, and Regina's mom happened to be home. "Reggie and Junior? Oh, my God!"

Every other time the guys had come by her mom had been at work. That day, she finally had some time off, so she said she wanted some new pictures to add to her collection from when they were younger. Reggie and Junior agreed, and Regina savored every moment of posing with the two men.

Her mom posted the pictures to her social media account, and Regina saved a few to print out at a local drug store and keep in her diary, too. She picked the best one of her and Reggie, and also the best one of her and Junior, despite the fact that Junior was her second choice. She carefully taped the photos to some blank pages of her diary so they wouldn't fall out. It was so exciting to have two men in her life, despite the fact that Marlena had to fuck up her chances with Reggie.

Then an idea came to mind. What if Reggie only messed with Marlena because Regina hadn't said anything? Regina and Reggie had often flirted with each other during their friendship. What if that was Reggie's way of saying he had feelings for her? What if Regina had simply moved too slow? She decided she was going to take a chance. She planned to tell Reggie her feelings the next time they saw each other, then let the chips fall where they may.

Unfortunately, the next time they saw each other, Reggie started acting standoffish. Regina had no idea why, but she later learned that Marlena had broken up with him. Then Regina heard the reason for the breakup was the picture they had taken together. Someone had sent it to Marlena's inbox saying Reggie was cheating with Regina.

Bitch! And if he was? So what? Regina thought to herself when Reggie told her this. Reggie didn't flirt with her anymore after that. Strike two for Marlena.

***

Despite the letdown from the fact that Reggie wasn't feeling her like she thought he was, Shaniqua left Red Lobster feeling good about his proposition. This plan wasn't too bad. It was easy money. All she had to do was befriend this chick named Marlena, get in good with her, then start scheming on her man, Junior.

Wasn't shit she wasn't used to, so Shaniqua was ready.

The next day, however, she received a death threat via a text message from the last guy she had blackmailed, Rell. It scared Shaniqua shitless, despite the fact that her gut told her Rell wasn't going to make good on his threat.

She wanted to lay low for a while in case her gut was wrong, but she'd already taken the money from Reggie.

Her gut told her Reggie wouldn't be the type to let her give the money back and renege.

Chapter 10

Pretty soon, it became clear to Regina that Reggie wasn't going to come around. She'd started dressing more stylishly when he and Junior came to chill. She'd applied light makeup here and there to accentuate her features. Regina had done everything she could, but still, it seemed that Reggie was not budging.

Then he popped up with a whole other bitch and pissed her clean off. Some bitch named Samia. She didn't have shit on Regina, in her opinion. Bitch was a six at best, while Regina stood at a seven. Eight with her makeup.

Regina could not stand the fact that she had lost out on love again.

After writing in her diary furiously for weeks, Regina decided it was time to cut her losses and focus on Junior.

She was pulling out all the stops this time. There was no way Junior was going to get the chance to turn her down like Reggie had. He was her man. Regina had this in the bag.

Until one day, Reggie mentioned something about a double date.

"Double date?" Regina snorted. "With who?"

She fully expected Reggie to say the double date was going to be with one of Samia's friends and her man.

It wasn't, though. It was with Junior and Marlena.

Regina's head was spinning when she heard this. "Junior and Marlena? Your ex, Marlena? And you're okay with this?" Her eyes narrowed, searching Reggie's for any hint that he was upset.

Reggie shrugged. "Bitch was fair game. I'm with Samia now."

"What about the bro code?" Regina shot back. She couldn't help but ask.

Reggie shrugged again. "I mean, I really don't give a fuck what Marlena does, to be honest. If she wants to choose a lesser man, so be it."

That, Regina could agree with. Junior was the lesser man in her eyes as well.

Yet in still, Marlena had stolen yet another man from under her nose before she could sink her teeth into him.

Strike three. Marlena was out.

***

Befriending Marlena was almost too easy for Shaniqua. All she had to do was send her a friend request, start liking her photos and commenting under her statuses on social media, and the two became fast friends.

The friendship was so seamless that Shaniqua accidentally revealed to Marlena that she was transgender the first time they hung out.

She clapped her hand over her mouth as soon as the words came out.

Marlena gave her a look of understanding, however.

"Wow, girl. That was huge." Marlena covered Shaniqua's hand with hers.

Her eyes were so compassionate, Shaniqua almost burst into tears. For what felt like the first time in her life, someone wasn't disgusted with her. Her mom wasn't disgusted, but Shaniqua never felt that she fully accepted her identity. She definitely loved Shaniqua, but Shaniqua could tell she only went along with her wishes because she didn't want to lose her, and not because she fully embraced her.

Marlena was different, however. She was proving herself to be a true friend, despite only knowing Shaniqua for a short period of time.

Shaniqua felt horrible for what she had been paid to do, but she got the shock of her life when Marlena actually approached her with a proposition of her own one day.

"Listen, girl. I have a question for you," she began.

Shaniqua perked up because she knew whatever the question was, it was huge.

Marlena's eyes clouded, and Shaniqua's heart went out to her.

"What is it, Mar?" she asked.

Marlena blinked back her tears. "I think Junior might be cheating."

Shaniqua grew hot. "Why do you think that?" She was ready to go to bat for Marlena against Junior, just based on hearing this news. Suddenly, however, Marlena looked unsure of the statement she just made.

"Well, maybe he's not, but I just don't feel like I can trust him."

"Why not?" Shaniqua pressed.

Marlena opened up and told her about how a year into her and Junior's relationship, he cheated on her and got some girl pregnant.

"The only reason I found out was because of the baby!" Marlena cried.

Shaniqua handed her a tissue.

Marlena dabbed her eyes, sniffled, then continued. "She ended up losing it, and he swore he would never do it again, but Shaniqua... I can't stand the fucking flashbacks. I hate feeling like this because I really love him, and I want us to work out."

They remained silent for a few moments. Shaniqua was unsure what she should say.

Marlena turned to her again after staring into space. "Do you think you can help me?"

Shaniqua opened her mouth to say no, then closed it. She remembered that cold, dark look in Reggie's eyes, as well as the reason she and Marlena became friends in the first place.

"Yes, girl," Shaniqua said. "I'll help you."

Chapter 11

Regina was beside herself with fury over the fact that Marlena had easily gotten with both Reggie and Junior. This bitch needed to be knocked down a peg or two. How dare she think she could just get with not one, but both of Regina's crushes?

Regina was the one who had longevity with Reggie and Junior. Not Marlena!

This bitch was gonna pay, she could believe that.

Regina found herself scouring Marlena's friends list until the wee hours of the morning. Marlena wasn't the only one who could get a man. She wasn't the only one who could make him fall head over heels. All Regina had to do was find a nigga that was close to Marlena, and then her plan would begin...

She found him. Corey.

When she first clicked on Corey's page, it was only because she noticed that Corey and Marlena had tons of mutual friends. That was how she judged that they must have been close to each other. After looking through Corey's statuses, she found that he and Marlena often reacted or commented on each other's posts.

Then she looked through Corey's pictures, and that was how she found out they were cousins. The evil grin she was wearing on her face grew.

"Show time," she said to herself.

It was easy for Shaniqua to get in contact with Junior because Marlena told her he always hung out at the arcades.

"He's just like a little damn kid," Marlena said, half blushing and half out of frustration. Shaniqua could tell her feelings were still mixed about her plan.

Although she still had the threat of Reggie hanging over her head, Shaniqua figured she had enough cash on her from the three guys she messed with to skip town if need be. She decided to make sure Marlena was sure she wanted her to go through with this before she went after Junior.

"Girl... are you prepared for whatever may happen by the end of this?" she asked.

The expression on Marlena's face told her she wasn't, but she nodded to say yes, anyway. "Yes, Shaniqua. I need to know."

Shaniqua's heart burned. She'd never been in a serious relationship herself, but she felt Marlena's pain. She just wanted to know if her man had truly changed.

Shaniqua hoped like hell that he had, but then that would be bad news for her. Reggie had been hitting her up every few days asking how the plan was going. He really wanted Junior to pay for whatever he had done to him.

Shaniqua never asked why Reggie wanted revenge so bad. First of all, it wasn't her place, and secondly, she figured the less she knew, the better.

Shaniqua looked up all the games at the arcade that Junior frequented, then she went to a separate arcade over the course of a week to prepare for their first encounter.

When she was finally ready, Marlena texted her to let her know Junior was there one day. Shaniqua went there and immediately spotted him. She had to admit the man was fine. He wasn't as fine as Reggie, but he was tall, caramel skinned, and had some juicy lips. Shaniqua definitely wouldn't mind giving him her body if it went that far.

She watched him for a few moments. He didn't notice her since he was totally engrossed in his game.

Finally, she approached him. "You look like you're doing good against the computer, but I bet you twenty dollars I could dust your ass."

She held up the twenty for emphasis as Junior turned to her.

His face broke out in a grin. His eyes checked her out, but he quickly refocused. "A'ight, bet," he said, licking his lips. He pulled out his own twenty and put it on the round table next to their game. Shaniqua did the same with hers. It was a racing car game they were playing, and Shaniqua had already looked up some secret cheat codes you could use to give yourself an advantage.

She used the codes sporadically throughout the game so Junior wouldn't suspect anything. They played three rounds, and Shaniqua let Junior win the first one, pretending to be disappointed, then she won the second and third.

"Mm mm mm," she mused. "Like taking candy from a baby."

Junior nodded at her in admiration. "You're nice as hell at this. I've never seen a female come in here by herself. How long have you been into arcades?"

His grin was making her kind of breathless, so Shaniqua found herself having to refocus now. Reggie's sexiness hit her in the face immediately. Junior's sexiness was the kind that crept up on her. It was hitting Shaniqua from all angles now.

She found herself silently hoping he took the bait. She might even fuck him twice.

She put a hair behind her ear and blushed to begin her flirt session. "Oh, I don't do it often. I used to when I was younger, but I just recently picked it back up."

Junior looked even more impressed. "Deadass? You just started back?"

Shaniqua nodded, feeling good about herself, even though she was totally lying. "Yeah, but you're pretty good, too." She reached out and touched his arm as she spoke.

He was attracted to her, she could tell, but the fact that he stepped back slightly told her where he stood.

"I always try to get my girl to come with me, but she's never interested."

Damn! Shaniqua's mind screamed. *Every single time I develop a crush...*

"Your girl? Damn, are y'all serious?" she asked the question to do her due diligence on Junior's character, but her gut already told her what his answer would be.

He nodded with another smile. "Yeah, we definitely are. That's my little baby."

"Damn, that sucks." Shaniqua chuckled as if to play it off. "Well, I'm not the type of woman to try to overstep a beautiful relationship. I believe in Black love, but can we still be friends, though?"

To her surprise, Junior accepted.

"Sure, that's cool!" he said. He pulled out his phone, and they exchanged numbers.

Shaniqua walked out of that arcade more conflicted than she'd ever been in her life.

After that day, she and Junior met up at the arcade a few times a week, and he kept his word about being true to his woman, never accepting her subtle advances.

Meanwhile, both Marlena and Reggie were blowing up her phone, asking how their plans were going.

Each of them was determined, but for completely opposite reasons.

Shaniqua had some decisions to make.

Chapter 12

Something told Shaniqua she was going down a dark path, but she ignored it. She found herself creating a fake profile for Junior's social media page, using his name and photo, then sending messages back and forth to herself to make it seem that Junior was flirting with her. She then sent those screenshots to both Reggie and Marlena.

She didn't like lying to her newfound friend because it really seemed like Marlena was genuine, but Reggie was scary as hell. She had to appease him.

Marlena grew more hurt and angrier by the day, while Reggie grew more elated.

"Hell yeah!" Reggie said when Shaniqua sent him screenshots of Junior supposedly asking her favorite sexual positions. "Keep that nigga going, then we pounce." Shaniqua didn't exactly know what Reggie meant by the word pounce, but she would soon find out.

Marlena, on the other hand, was absolutely heartbroken. She didn't portray what she was feeling to her man, from what she told Shaniqua, but she was on the brink of doing so.

That put Shaniqua in a difficult position. Reggie had to go ahead and do whatever the hell he was about to do to Junior before Marlena found out the truth.

***

Regina stalked Corey for weeks before she finally put herself in a position to be seen by him. She knew all his hangout spots, all his friends, where he worked, everything.

Getting him to approach her was easy as hell.

All she had to do was put on a little makeup, show a little skin, and she was set.

Corey's jaw practically dropped to the floor when he first saw her.

"Hey," he said when she eyed him as they walked past each other. She was on her way into one of his favorite food joints, while he was on his way out.

She looked back at him, pretending to blush like she was shy. "Hey." Then she looked down at the ground.

"What's your name?" Corey asked.

Regina looked back up at him. "Regina. What's yours?"

He smiled and stepped closer. "Corey. Regina is a pretty name. Reminds me of royalty."

Regina smiled for real this time. *That's right, nigga,* she thought. *Recognize me for the queen I am.* She knew from Corey's statuses that he'd recently broken up with his girlfriend, so she planned on being the best rebound he could have ever imagined.

"Thank you," she said as she stepped closer to him in order to give off the impression that she was gaining confidence, but it was really so he would catch a whiff of her perfume, the same kind that he'd posted his ex-girlfriend wore. She knew the Christian Dior would work its magic. The sad look that crossed Corey's features let her know she had her way in. He was still vulnerable.

She reached out and gently touched his arm. "What's wrong?"

Corey licked his lips, then shook his head. "Nothing. That's a beautiful scent. Christian Dior, right?"

Corey sounded nervous, but Regina knew she had him right where she wanted.

She smiled. "That's right!"

"How about I buy your lunch?" Corey asked.

Regina's smile widened. "That sounds great."

***

Corey felt like he'd met the woman of his dreams. He thought he was in love with Ashley, his ex, but Regina was proving to give her a run for her money already.

It felt like Regina knew him better than he knew himself. She finished his sentences, understood the way he thought, and made him feel loved and cherished, something Ashley never quite did.

It seemed Corey had finally found the one.

Everyone always said that nice guys finished last, but Corey didn't care about that, as long as he finished with Regina.

Chapter 13

It had only been a few weeks since Corey started dating Regina, but it felt like a match made in heaven. They connected on a deep level. It felt like they knew each other spiritually.

Plus, her sex game was on point. Regina could twist her limbs in all types of angles that Corey had never even heard of. Not to mention, that little trick she did with her tongue.

He remembered their first encounter.

Regina had invited him over for dinner. Corey was nervous at first because although they had hit it off pretty well so far, their relationship was still very new.

Part of his mind told him he didn't really know Regina that well, which was true since they'd literally just met less than a month prior, but another part of him said this was the real thing.

He'd finally found that one woman who he could settle down with. Far cry from Ashley's burning ass. She fucked one of his boys and caused a lifelong friendship to go down the drain. Then, when she found that the grass wasn't greener on the other side, she wanted to come back to Corey. Fuck that. Bitch could stay that way. Her and her gonorrhea.

Regina was different, and Corey could already tell from how clean she kept her apartment, as well as the mouthwatering scent of the food she was cooking.

Corey's eyes were on Regina's behind as her hips swayed back and forth. She was leading him to the kitchen to eat the dinner she prepared but looking at how her ass bounced in that royal blue halter dress, he wanted to make a pit stop in the hallway and eat something else.

He didn't see a panty line, but she might have been wearing a thong. Either way, he would have easy access.

He moved to grab her arm and turn her body to face him, but he chickened out. He didn't want Regina to think he was a creep.

They entered the kitchen, and Regina finally turned back to face him with a smile. "I didn't cook much," she said with a seductive, yet shy grin that drove Corey insane. "Just some plantains and oxtails with gravy. I did them in the crockpot. I hope you don't mind."

"Why would I mind?" Corey asked, his mouth watering for more than one thing.

Regina shrugged. "Oh, just because this was my first time making them, and I wasn't sure how to. I low key burnt the cabbage. I made that part on the stove."

"I'm sure it's alright," Corey said, not giving a fuck about that food, especially since he could now see that Regina wasn't wearing a bra, either. Her nipples stood at attention. Corey was mesmerized.

Damn, what I would give... he thought, then he snapped out of it. Regina was waving her hand in front of his face.

"Corey? I said, did you want me to include the cabbage on your plate since it got burnt?"

"Huh? Oh, yeah, go ahead," he said, tearing his eyes away from Regina's bosom to take in the interior of her kitchen. It was tiny, but not in a cramped way. She had a good amount of counter space, a stainless-steel refrigerator and stove, and a wooden table and chairs. Her decorations were pink and white. *Pretty good taste,* Corey thought to himself. He pulled out a chair and sat as Regina placed his plate and utensils before him. Then she pulled out a bottle of Don Julio from the fridge. "Drink?" she asked with another smile.

Corey nodded his approval and watched her pour it into a glass filled with ice. *How she know that's my shit?* he thought.

Regina sat the glass before him, and Corey wasted no time digging in.

He barely noticed Regina wasn't eating her plate as he devoured his. Those oxtails were out of this world, and he couldn't even tell the cabbage was burnt. Regina was going to be his wife. It was already decided.

"Damn, ma," Corey said as he finished the last of his glass of Don Julio and Regina jumped up to pour him another.

He was drinking the second glass when he saw Regina pick up a pack of Halls throat lozenges from her counter and pop one in her mouth.

"Oh, no. Are you sick?" Corey asked. His mind was swimming due to the alcohol, but he was still concerned for his woman. Well, she wasn't his woman yet, but she would be. He knew it with his soul.

He and Regina were meant to be.

Regina didn't answer his question. She just moved the throat lozenge around in her mouth in a seductive fashion.

Corey finished his second drink around the same time she finished with her medicine, or so he thought.

"Listen, Regina, if you're not feeling well, I don't want to put you out..." Corey began, but a wicked grin grew across Regina's features.

"I'm not sick, silly," she finally answered and walked up on him.

Her hands were unfastening his belt before he could realize what was happening.

"Regina..." His body wanted what he thought she was about to do, but he didn't want to take advantage of her. "You don't have to do this," he told her, though his mind was screaming at him to shut the fuck up.

Regina now had his mans out of his boxers, standing at full attention.

She was on her knees, but then she looked back up at Corey. "You sure?" she asked. "If I stop, how are we going to get rid of this?"

The moment her tiny hands gripped him Corey knew it was over.

He said not another word as Regina proceeded to blow his mind.

When she finished, Corey could not contain himself. "Marry me! Please, Regina."

She just chuckled in response.

***

Corey's ass was lightweight. Regina told him she was going to the bathroom to brush her teeth, but it was really to gloat over the fact that she got him that easy.

By the time she was finished, neither Corey nor Marlena would know that hit them.

"Watch me work, bitch," she whispered to herself in the mirror.

Chapter 14

Shaniqua finally understood that Reggie was way more sadistic than she thought. She listened with increasing fear and apprehension as Reggie laid out his plan of kidnapping and murder.

He looked at her when he was finished like he expected her to congratulate him on a job well done or something. "What do you think?" Reggie asked after a few moments of Shaniqua's silence.

Shaniqua racked her brains for an adequate response. "Um... So, you're saying you want me to help you kidnap him? Reggie, I don't really have experience with this sort of thing."

Reggie's features softened as he reassured her. "Oh, don't worry about that, ma. I'm gonna be doing most of the dirty work. Once he's at your crib, he's all mine. I mainly just need you to do a little seduction and possibly a little driving."

Shaniqua opened her mouth, ready to try to inch her way out of this arrangement, when Reggie cut back in.

"Don't forget. I paid you very well to do your job."

There was that darkness again. Shaniqua had almost forgotten how cold Reggie's eyes could get. She fought not to shudder as she became transfixed once again by the darkness of his pupils.

"I gotchu," she managed to squeak out before she excused herself, lying and saying she was running late for a hair appointment.

***

Reggie watched as Shaniqua got into her car and peeled off from their meeting place. He couldn't believe her nerve.

"I gave this bitch six racks and now she wants to renege?" His trigger finger was itching, but he had a feeling Shaniqua would follow through with his plan.

Still, he felt like he needed a backup.

Reggie racked his brains for a few moments before his features lit up.

"Regina..." he said with a smile, then went to her name in his contacts.

***

Regina could not believe it when Reggie's sexy face popped up on her screen with not a text, but a call!

Usually, if Reggie contacted her, it was to respond to a text she'd sent him days or weeks prior. She was beginning to think he didn't want her friendship anymore.

Reggie had quit his job at the factory a few weeks ago, so Regina was stuck looking in Junior's face every day.

Not that she had a problem with Junior, outside of the fact that he dissed her for that bitch Marlena.

But now, Reggie was calling her, and Regina was damn sure going to answer.

"Hello?" she said, trying to sound as soft and airy as possible.

"Hey," Reggie said, his voice low, deep, and seductive.

Regina perked up immediately. Usually, his tone was bored or distracted. Why the sudden change? Had he finally seen the light? Regina was so excited she was ready to kick herself.

"What are you doing?" she asked.

"Nothing much. I just wanted to stop by to see you tonight. Is your mom home?"

Regina's stomach was doing somersaults now. He was asking if her mom was home. This could only mean one thing. She hoped it did. She prayed it did.

Fuck Corey's soft ass. Reggie was a real man.

"Um, no, she's not home. What time did you want to come through?" Regina tried to sound sweet and sultry when she said those words to let Reggie know she was down for whatever.

His response told her he got the message.

"Shit, I can be on my way right now."

Regina almost broke character. "Okay, see you soon."

She hung up and stared at her phone screen, frozen in place for a few moments. Then, she sprang into action. This was the moment she had been waiting for. She had to get ready for her man.

Regina pulled out all the stops.

She went to the back of her closet for her sluttiest lingerie. She had purchased it months ago in preparation for if she'd ever gotten a chance with Reggie. She also went to the folder she had saved in her phone exclusively for him. The folder contained pictures of a hair style, makeup selection, and notes on what she would do and say when Reggie finally recognized her as his woman.

She got her body, hair, and face right while she rehearsed her lines over and over.

She'd already GPS'd the distance from Reggie's house to her house in the past so she knew if he was coming from home, he would be there in no more than ten minutes.

Regina took a few more deep breaths and began rehearsing again, then she heard a knock on her front door.

She peered out the window of her bedroom, which faced the front of the apartment she shared with her mom, and immediately got pissed.

"Corey? What the fuck are you doing here?"

Chapter 15

Corey stood outside Regina's apartment, clutching the arrangement of pink roses in his hand, along with a nice card, which declared his feelings for her, and a box of customized chocolates. Regina wasn't expecting him, but Corey wanted to pop up on his baby and surprise her.

She popped up in his life in the form of a surprise and blessing, so Corey longed to return the favor.

He knocked on her door again, hoping he wasn't waking her out of her sleep or something. He saw her car parked in the lot, so he knew she was home. Why wasn't she answering?

Corey knocked again, then his phone buzzed in his pocket with a call from Regina.

"Hello?" he answered.

She was silent on the other line. Corey took the phone away from his ear to make sure the call wasn't dropped. It wasn't. He tried again. "Hey, baby. How are you?"

"Hey," Regina answered, her voice low and gravelly. Something was wrong. Corey's heart panged with apprehension.

"Baby, what happened? Are you okay?"

"No..." Regina hacked on the other end like she was coughing up a huge glob of phlegm. Corey jumped at the sudden and forceful sound. His baby wasn't doing too good at all. "I think I came down with something," she finally said.

"Let me come in," he offered. "I'm actually standing outside your front door."

"No. Corey, I don't want you catching this," Regina huffed. "I already got some medicine. I'm just going to take a few days."

"Baby, at least let me see your face," he said. "I brought you some flowers."

"Oh, thank you. That's so sweet. Just leave them in the mailbox. I'll get them later. The doctor says I'm really contagious, so I don't want to get you sick, too."

Corey wanted to press it, but he could tell Regina really didn't want him seeing her all sick. He wouldn't mind. He was ready and willing to take care of her, but if she didn't want to see him while she was sick, he would be understanding.

"Okay, baby," he said finally. "I'll call you later tonight to check in. Anything you need, you call me, and I will come flying over. No questions asked."

"Thank you so much," Regina said in a weak voice.

Corey gently placed the flowers into the mailbox and propped the top open so they wouldn't get crushed. He also arranged the chocolates and card so they would be seen as well. Then he got in his car and drove back home.

***

Regina sucked her teeth and rolled her eyes as she saw Corey driving off. "Fina-damn-ly," she breathed, then she bounded out of her room to go and grab the flowers out of the mailbox.

She retrieved them, along with the chocolates and card.

Her heart panged when she thought of the care Corey had put into these gifts. Only for a second, though. Regina was a woman on a mission, and no one was stopping her, even if Corey did have good intentions.

She stuffed the flowers into the trashcan in her kitchen and pushed them down so Reggie wouldn't see them.

Regina loved chocolates, however. They were the expensive kind, too, and somehow Corey had selected all her favorite flavors. "Guess I'm not the only one who knows how to research," Regina mused as she read the back of the box. She put the chocolates in the freezer behind the frozen meats and vegetables so they would be hidden. As for the card, she decided she'd read it later. She put it in her diary and stuffed it under the floorboard in her bedroom just as another knock on her door sounded.

Regina tripped and banged her shin against the metal corner of her bed frame as she ran toward her bedroom window, praying it wasn't Corey again. "Ow!" she whimpered, fighting back tears and hoping the pain subsided soon.

The knocking sounded again. Regina hobbled over to the window, ready to curse Corey out this time for making her hurt herself. She told his ass to leave.

Thankfully, it wasn't Corey standing outside her door this time, though.

Reggie was here.

Suddenly, the pain in Regina's shin faded away as a smile grew on her features.

"Showtime!" she said, shimmying her shoulders before prancing to open the door.

Chapter 16

Reggie always had a feeling about Regina. When they worked together at the factory, he used to catch her staring at him like she wanted him.

If he was honest with himself, Reggie didn't think Regina was that bad looking. She was fuckable, at least, and that was what he intended to do tonight, fuck her silly, then get her in on his plan.

As soon as she opened the door, Reggie wasted no time. He had come over in his grey sweatpants, white wifebeater, and white socks with black Adidas slides.

Reggie liked to call it his thot-fit. He wore this same getup whenever he was attending to one of his bitches.

Regina wasn't one of his bitches yet, but she would be after tonight.

Regina's eyes popped open when Reggie grabbed her up in his muscular embrace, but before she could say a word, his lips were devouring hers.

Reggie felt her hands pressing against his chest after a few moments, so he eased back slightly, breaking the kiss.

"Damn," Regina said, her expression hazy like she was already open for him. "Baby, let me close the door first, at least."

Reggie smirked and stepped to the side so Regina could secure her apartment. Then, she grabbed his hand and led him to her bedroom.

Reggie's eyes swept over Regina's body as they walked. She was wearing some sexy lingerie. *Damn, she must really be feeling a nigga.* He gave himself props.

His mind briefly went back to earlier days when he wasn't considered sexy or popular. When he was in elementary and middle school, Reggie was always teased due to being shorter and scrawnier than the other guys.

Once he hit high school, however, all that stopped.

Reggie sprang up a full foot over the course of the summer, and in his freshman year, he towered over all the other freshmen. Junior passed him in height in sophomore year, but they both continued to grow taller into their junior year.

By the time they graduated, Junior was still taller, but Reggie was more muscular.

That was why he got way more bitches.

Junior crossed the line when he stole Marlena from him. He could have had any other woman, but he stepped to his boy's girl. Reggie didn't see that as something he could come back from.

He suspected there was some bullshit behind the scenes when Marlena broke up with him out of nowhere, claiming she had proof he was cheating.

When he told Junior the story, the look in his eyes told Reggie he already knew, but Reggie had no way to prove it.

That night Marlena left her phone at his house, it was all revealed.

And that was why Junior's ass had to die.

Reggie watched as Regina practically flung herself onto her bed. She was almost a little too thirsty for him, but this was all business, anyway.

Reggie slowly removed his wifebeater and sweatpants, stepping out of his slides so all he wore were his boxers and socks.

From the way Regina's eyes widened at the sight of his package, which was barely concealed beneath the thin fabric of his boxers, Reggie knew this was about to be a lit night.

He climbed into the bed and got on top of her.

***

Regina could not believe this moment had finally come. The sexual chemistry between she and Reggie had been burning for eons. It was high time they finally let it loose.

She decided she was pulling out all stops tonight. She was going to make her mark on Reggie and leave him begging her for more.

Regina's moans grew louder, and her center grew wetter as Reggie kissed, licked, and caressed her in all the right places.

When he flipped their positions so that she was on top, she was more than ready to return the favor. She kissed and licked him, too, starting with his right ear down to his neck. She focused on his Adam's apple for a few since that seemed to give him more pleasure. When her lips and tongue found their way to his left nipple, he gently pushed her shoulder back.

"What?" she asked, giving him a coy look.

Reggie's lower lip trembled. "Come on, ma."

She shot him a devilish smile and ignored him, circling her tongue around his nipple, then gently biting it.

Reggie's response let her know that this was one of his spots. She did the same to his other nipple, and he enjoyed that, too, but it didn't have the same effect as the first one.

Finally, she trailed lower, grabbing his boxers and trying to pull them down.

Reggie grabbed her hands. "Pause," he said.

"What?" Regina said again.

"You not about to do me like I'm some chick." He chuckled.

Regina laughed and got off him so he could remove his own boxers, while she removed her lingerie.

Now, they were both naked with the exception of Reggie's socks. The thought crossed Regina's mind to take them off so she could lick his toes, but from the way he had responded thus far, she decided against it. She would save that trick for another time.

Regina resumed action, focusing on his huge and pulsing member.

Reggie's vocal and physical responses let her know she was on the right track. The way he was pushing her head down almost made her uncomfortable, but at the same time, she loved it.

When he climaxed, Regina went to the bathroom to wash her mouth out, then returned to her bed. Reggie was on his cell phone. It looked like he was scrolling through social media or something.

Regina's heart dropped. She thought Reggie would be enraptured by their time together, as she was. Maybe she shouldn't have gone to the bathroom.

Reggie looked at her and put his phone on her nightstand.

Regina got back on top of him and moved to kiss him, but he quickly flipped their positions so he was on top. He didn't kiss her lips this time, but he kissed her neck, then went down to her nipples, returning her previous favor to him.

Regina moaned and gently pushed his head to get him to go lower, but he didn't.

Instead, he rose back up to face her, then proceeded to inch her legs apart further so he could assume his position.

When he entered her, it took Regina's breath away. She'd heard so many stories about Reggie's sex game from the girls who he'd slept with at the factory, but they didn't say it was like this.

Reggie knew exactly what to do and when to do it.

By the end of the night, Regina was satisfied.

Chapter 17

Regina always envisioned her and Reggie cuddling after their first time together, but Reggie's abrupt change in demeanor told her that wasn't happening. He was back to sitting on the side of the bed, staring at the wall, but looking like he was about to ask her something.

She reached for him, but pulled her hand back, deciding against the attempt at intimacy.

Reggie turned to face her. "Let me ask you something."

"What is it?" Regina asked, her heart pounding wildly. She hoped this was the moment she had been waiting for. Was Reggie going to make her his girl?

"How would you like to do me a favor?"

Regina's hopes faltered, just like that. *A favor?* After the beautiful night they just shared with the crescendos caused by their lovemaking, Reggie was asking for a favor?

"What kind of favor, Reggie?"

Reggie's features softened, like he noticed her offense.

He licked his lips. "Come on, ma. I know that you are the only woman I can ask something like this. You've always been a rider."

Regina felt herself perking up again. If Reggie considered her a rider, that meant there was still hope. "What's the favor?"

She listened as Reggie explained. She was shocked at his idea to kidnap his best friend to teach him a lesson, but she loved the idea of getting under Marlena's skin in the process. That bitch definitely deserved to be taught a lesson.

Regina nodded to agree with the plan. "Yes, I'll do it."

Reggie smiled. "You will?"

Regina traced a finger up his muscular forearm. "You know I gotchu, baby. I'm your rider."

Reggie chuckled. "That, you are, and maybe after this is over we can see about me and you."

Regina wasn't sure if she'd heard him correctly. "You're serious?"

Reggie nodded. "As a heart attack."

***

The next part of Regina's plan with Corey had been repurposed, due to her conversation with Reggie. Corey was already gullible and vulnerable. Convincing him of his precious cousin Marlena's culpability would be easy work.

She decided to do it one night while they were watching a movie. Regina mustered up some crocodile tears when it ended, and Corey immediately jumped to comfort her.

"What's wrong?" he asked.

She sniffled. "Nothing. Just thinking about some of the things I've been through."

Corey was all ears. "What kinds of things, baby? You can talk to me."

Regina's expression darkened as if she was unsure. "I'm not sure you would want to know."

"Why you say that?"

"Because..." She chose her words carefully. "It's about your cousin."

Corey looked confused. "My cousin?" He wrinkled his nose.

Regina clarified. "I saw on your page that Marlena is your cousin."

Corey smiled. "Yeah, that's my girl. My ace. Me and Marlena are thick as thieves."

Regina was silent.

"What happened between you and her?"

She remained quiet to get him to urge her to continue.

"Come on, baby," Corey persisted.

Regina sighed. "She got me fired."

"Got you fired? When did y'all work together?"

Regina swallowed. "When I graduated high school, I started working at a movie theater. I was struggling heavy, and this job was my only income. I was barely making enough to get by. Marlena worked there, too, and she used to bully me."

Corey's eyes widened. "Bully you? How so?"

"My job was as one of the ushers, but Marlena didn't like to work, so she wanted to be an usher in my place. She convinced the managers to have us switch spots. With ushers, the job was mainly to clean out the theaters after movies ended, and some of us would also take tickets. It was the easier job, and most of the day we spent goofing off and watching movies."

Corey looked like he was thinking back. "Yeah, I do remember Marlena working at the movies."

Regina became nervous. Her next question was a critical one. "Did you tell Marlena about me and you being together?"

Corey shook his head like the good boy Regina knew he was. "No, I haven't told anyone. I know you said you wanted to take things slow and keep it in the cut. I can't wait to introduce you to my family, though. My mom would love you."

Regina didn't have the heart to tell Corey she would never be meeting his mother. Once she was done with this plan, she was dropping him and moving on with Reggie.

Corey was a sweet guy. He would find someone else.

"Good." she smiled. "I just get a little nervous about speaking on things too soon."

"Finish the story," Corey said, looking a little testy.

Regina wondered what upset him all of a sudden, then she figured he was still mad about the fact that their relationship was being kept a secret.

"Anyway," she sighed. "Marlena ended up getting me fired. I was working at the concession counter, selling the popcorn and snacks and all that stuff. Large amounts of money started missing from the drawers, and management was cracking down on us. Marlena didn't like me, and she was already bullying me, anyway, so she convinced a few of the other concession workers to go to the managers and say I was the one stealing. They set me up, shorting my register one day when I wasn't paying attention. I ended up getting fired. The company took the missing money out of my last paycheck, so I didn't even have enough to pay my rent."

Regina forced out another tear since this was supposed to be a sad story.

Corey looked like he felt for her. "Marlena really did that?"

She nodded. "She did. I couldn't find another job in time, so I ended up getting evicted. I was homeless for a minute because I was too ashamed to go back to my mom's house after getting my own place. I finally humbled myself after getting my job at the factory, and I have been living with my mom ever since."

Corey was silent for a moment after Regina's story finished. She let the silence linger, hoping her lie would marinate as truth in his mind.

"Damn, baby. I'm so sorry to hear what she did to you. I've never known Marlena to be a grimy person."

Regina felt herself getting upset. He didn't believe her? Fuck that. She was pulling out all stops. "Well, Corey, she might be a good person in other ways, but when it comes to female shit? Marlena is a different story. She's one of the reasons I want to keep our relationship a secret, honestly."

"You think she would try to mess us up?"

Regina nodded like she felt vulnerable. "Or turn your mom and the rest of the family against me, like she did the people at our job."

Corey nodded like he understood. *Thank God*, Regina thought. *He's biting the bait.*

Once Corey was convinced of Marlena causing Regina's homelessness, it was a piece of cake to get him in on a little plan for revenge.

Regina carefully constructed her argument to get Corey on board to text Marlena and tell her that her boyfriend was sleeping with another woman. Then he was going to drop the bomb. That the woman had HIV. Of course, it was a lie, but it was designed to take something from Marlena like Marlena took something from Regina. Marlena would lose her boyfriend, like Regina lost her job.

Thankfully, Corey agreed with the logic.

***

When Corey initially heard Regina's plan, it made him feel a little uneasy. He understood her wanting to get back at Marlena for what she had done, but still, Marlena was his cousin.

Regina was his girl, however, and he was head over heels for her.

When Regina showed him screenshots of a conversation between Marlena's boyfriend, Junior, and a girl named Shaniqua, Corey decided to go through with it.

On his end, yes, Regina would get her revenge, but more importantly, his cousin would get rid of a fuck nigga.

Marlena was in love with Junior, so it would hurt, but in Corey's opinion, it was better for her to hurt now and get over Junior's cheating than for her to stay with him and remain clueless, then hurt more down the road.

He was in.

Chapter 18

After Shaniqua finished her convoluted ass story of how she became involved with Reggie, Junior was pissed. Point blank, he got played. He should have known good and damn well nobody needed a computer fixed at three in the morning. He really thought Shaniqua was his friend, though.

Junior's current predicament of being tied up on the floor of an abandoned building was his fault for stealing his boy's girl and playing him, but still.

He deserved to die for it, though?

Junior didn't think so. He prayed with all his heart that he could somehow manage to get Reggie to change his mind or find a way to get Shaniqua to help him escape. Then he could get to Marlena and contact the police.

He tried to slowly, but subtly, swipe his blade against the rope that was holding his hands back, but every time Reggie turned his attention off him, he would turn right back. Junior was starting to lose hope, but something told him he was going to find a way out of here.

He looked at Shaniqua again as she and Reggie were talking. Something about the way she was acting told him she wasn't really down with what Reggie wanted to do, but it might have just been wishful thinking. She had helped to kidnap him, after all.

Maybe if he could somehow get Reggie to go away for a minute, he would have a chance to talk to Shaniqua privately. Maybe then she would help him break free.

In the meantime, he kept making slow and subtle movements, trying to work his blade.

***

Never fear, never fold, Reggie's mind told him. The way he had come up, his survival instincts were always on ready. Outside of the one body he previously revealed to Junior that he had dropped, Reggie actually had two more.

But those people were meaningless to him. Junior was his day one. Reggie wished he could rewind the clock for his friend to show him what the outcome of crossing him would be, but that was impossible. Plus, it was far too late. Junior knew how the fuck Reggie was built. While Junior was doing well in school, making A's and B's, Reggie was running the streets, stacking cash and fucking up his life. His one saving grace that allowed him to graduate high school was that since he and Junior shared classes together, Reggie would just copy his assignments, change a few answers, and put his name at the top. None of the teachers seemed to know or care. Their school wasn't shit, anyway, as the graduation rate was only thirty three percent. Junior wasn't the street type like Reggie, which meant he would go straight to the cops instead of just taking this situation as a lesson.

No, there could be no loose ends. Reggie couldn't let him go.

Once this was over, Reggie would just focus on the good times he and Junior shared as they were growing up.

***

Regina navigated past the city into a rundown, rural area. "What the fuck are they doing all the way out here?" she said to herself, then she thought it was brilliant.

If Junior tried to scream or something, nobody would ever hear him out here. Wasn't shit but barns, waist high grass, and dilapidated wooden fences.

Finally, she came up to an area with three abandoned buildings spaced about a hundred yards apart from each other. She didn't see any cars parked out front, but if this was the address Shaniqua gave her, this was where she and Reggie were. Maybe their cars were parked out back or something. It could certainly be true, seeing that the buildings were wide and large. Each was the size of a multi bedroom house and maroon in color with rotted wood holding them together.

"This place looks like it smells like death warmed over," Regina told herself.

Then she looked down at her sandals. "I hope there ain't no snakes in this damn grass," she said to herself.

She sucked her teeth and pulled onto the grass, then got out, clicking her key fob to lock her doors.

"Showtime," she said to herself. Then she straightened out her dress and walked up toward building 1C where Shaniqua said they were located.

Chapter 19

When Shaniqua heard the sound of a car door locking outside, she almost let out a deep breath. Maybe Regina could help her talk some sense into Reggie's crazy ass. Shaniqua didn't know Regina prior to meeting Reggie, but once Reggie told Shaniqua he had someone watching her to make sure she did her job, Regina introduced herself.

Regina didn't seem that concerned with fucking with Shaniqua, though, and for that, she was grateful. It wouldn't take a rocket scientist to figure out that the profile Shaniqua was using to frame Junior was fake as fuck. All one had to do was look up his name and see multiple accounts, one of which only having one friend, Shaniqua.

Because of the fact that Regina wasn't on her like that, Shaniqua figured maybe she had a level head.

Reggie, on the other hand, looked pissed that somebody had pulled up to his not-so-secret location when he heard the car door lock.

"Who the fuck is that?" he asked, then he looked at Junior as if he was trying to figure out if Junior had somehow called someone. Then he turned to Shaniqua. "You watch him. I'm-a check this out."

Shaniqua's heart dropped.

Reggie walked outside, and Shaniqua backed up while still facing Junior so she could get a gauge of Regina and Reggie's conversation.

Regina felt nervous as she saw the door to the building open, and Reggie step outside. "Hey!" she said, flashing him a smile. He was looking sexy as hell with that wifebeater and those jeans, but the expression on his face was kind of scary.

"What the fuck are you doing here?" Reggie asked. "How'd you get this address?" He spat on the ground.

"Shaniqua gave it to me. She said to meet y'all here." Regina's heart was pounding in her chest. She hoped Reggie wasn't upset with her.

"Meet us here for what?" Reggie asked, his tone neutral.

Regina played with her hair. "I don't know. What's going on in there? I'm sure whatever y'all are doing, I could be of assistance."

A flash of something went through Reggie's eyes, but Regina couldn't call what it was. She still wasn't sure how Reggie felt about her pulling up here.

"I've been missing you," she said softly, trying to butter him up.

His features softened slightly. "Oh, yeah?"

"Yes. I can't wait until this is over so we can just do us."

Reggie took a step closer to her. "Do us, huh?"
"Yeah."

When he held her flirty gaze, Regina knew she had Reggie right where she wanted him.

He opened his arms to give her a hug, and she readily stepped into them. For a second there, Regina thought Reggie was going to reject her, and if he did, that would have been a problem. She was already jealous of the fact that Shaniqua was the one who got to be right next to him up to this point, but sooner or later, Shaniqua would learn her true place.

Reggie was Regina's man, not Shaniqua's.

Reggie held her tightly for a few seconds, then Regina pulled back to kiss him. She leaned up, but gasped as he roughly turned her around, his fingers quickly lacing around her neck.

Regina's mind was filled with shock as Reggie's thumbs pressed into the middle of her throat. She felt like he was crushing her windpipe.

Her arms flailed to get him to loosen up and stop playing, but after a few moments of struggling, she realized this wasn't a game.

Reggie wasn't playing.

He was going to kill her.

***

Shaniqua couldn't hear what Reggie and Regina were saying, but she hoped they hurried up and came inside so she could shoot Regina a hint or something to let her know they needed to end this shit.

She glanced back at Junior, who she realized was trying to get her attention.

"What?" she asked, taking a step closer to him.

"Shaniqua," he whispered. "You gotta help..."

Aggressive movement out of the corner of Shaniqua's eyes caught her attention.

The color drained from her face, and her jaw dropped as she watched Reggie strangling Regina to death with his bare hands.

"Oh, shit!" she hissed, clapping her hand back over her mouth.

She looked at Junior lying on the floor, then back at Reggie as Regina's body was sinking lower and lower to the ground as she lost consciousness.

Her arms were no longer flailing as they were before, but Reggie wasn't loosening his grip.

Finally, he let go, but from the way Regina's head lolled to the side, Shaniqua knew there was no way she was still alive.

Reggie sharply turned to face Shaniqua, and she practically jumped out of her skin.

The grin on his face made her sick to her stomach.

He walked back into the building, not taking his eyes off Shaniqua.

Shaniqua's eyes were shooting back and forth between Regina's body lying on the ground outside, and the crazed expression on Reggie's face.

"Reggie, what the hell?"

He shrugged, finally breaking eye contact and looking at the floor. "I had to see if I could do it," was all he said.

Do what? Shaniqua's mind screamed. What the hell was Reggie talking about?

His next words didn't give her any answers to that question. "Let me go take care of her. Thank God I made provisions for this sort of thing."

Chapter 20

Reggie couldn't believe he had done it. "Practice makes perfect," he mumbled under his breath, then went back outside the building to hoist Regina's body up on his shoulders. She was lightweight for Reggie, though his heart was still heavy.

Regina really believed she and Reggie were going to get married when he finished his plan with Junior.

She had confessed her love for him after the third time they had sex. Reggie was surprised when he heard those words because a female had never said that to him before, not even his mother.

Reggie's mother was hard as fuck on him as he was growing up, often punching him in the chest to toughen him up and burning his fingers on the rings of the stove when he got in trouble.

Reggie didn't get into too much trouble, at home at least, and his mother's plans to toughen him up so he wouldn't be like his *weak ass daddy* worked, but now Reggie often wondered if he was too tough for his own good.

Part of his mind told him that Regina didn't deserve what he had just done to her. He threw her body into the huge hole that he previously dug behind the building for Junior. They could probably both fit... if he still wanted to go through with this.

Reggie shook his head forcefully. Hell yeah, he was going through with this. He wasn't bitching up now.

Plus, he could still change his original plan for Junior's death and do the other one... then Junior wouldn't need to fit in the hole with Regina.

Reggie smiled at that thought. He had to admit, he liked his second plan better.

His momma didn't raise no pussies. That was what she often told him as she beat him with a whip and dared him to cry at thirteen, not satisfied until there were at least six welts on his back.

***

Corey pulled up to Regina's apartment, only to see that she wasn't there. He sucked his teeth. "Why would she practically curse me out for not being on time, then not be here when I got here?"

If he was honest with himself, Corey was getting sick of Regina's games. Yes, she was still his baby, and yes, he was still head over heels, but her recent behavior was making him suspicious.

Like the fact that she called him by another man's name the last time they had sex.

"Who the hell is Reggie?" Corey had asked, stopping mid-stroke.

Regina's face was flushed. "Um, nobody."

Corey pulled out, suddenly losing all interest in what could have previously been described as a mind-blowing sex session.

"What do you mean, nobody, Regina? Are you seeing someone else?"

Her eyes widened. "Baby, no! No, I would never do that to you."

Corey wasn't convinced. "If you are, Regina, you need to just tell me now."

"Corey, I'm not cheating." Regina looked like she was catching an attitude.

Corey decided to drop the issue. He didn't want to upset her, but that was a definite red flag. She kept urging him to get back into bed, but he said he was no longer in the mood.

Later that night, while Regina slept after they watched a movie together, Corey found himself installing a secret app on her phone that would track her location and transfer the information to the same app on his phone, including giving him access to all her text messages and inboxes.

He'd felt so bold as he installed it, saying to himself that he wasn't going out like he did with Ashley and that this was a preventative measure against Regina's cheating, but the next morning, he felt like he was kidding himself.

He wasn't some tough guy. He was a softie, which was why the saying went nice guys finished last.

Still, he hadn't used the app to check on Regina as of yet.

The fact that she wasn't home today, however, gave him pause. He decided to go to the app just to see where she was.

When he scrolled his phone and clicked on her location, he didn't recognize the address. It wasn't even in the same town.

Corey wrinkled his nose, but his gut told him something was off. He pressed the maps button on his phone. He was popping up today.

Chapter 21

Shaniqua revealed to Junior that Reggie killed Regina while Reggie was taking Regina's body out to the back.

"You gotta get me out of here," Junior pleaded. "Please, just help me get loose, and we can take him together."

Shaniqua swallowed, full of fear. "I can't."

"Come on!" Junior persisted. "If the nigga just killed Regina in cold blood, what the hell you think he's gonna do to me and you? Me and Regina grew up with Reggie. This is serious, Niqua."

Shaniqua looked like she was seriously considering it for a second, then she snapped to attention. "Hold on a second."

"Shaniqua..."

"Hold on!" she hissed, and walked over to a side door, unlocking it and opening it slightly. Junior watched as Shaniqua stared out the door to see what Reggie was doing, while he worked furiously to cut that fucking rope.

If he was able to break free before Shaniqua spotted him, Junior was knocking her on her ass. He didn't give a damn if she was a female at this point.

He got the rope halfway cut before Shaniqua suddenly closed the door and walked back to the middle of the floor.

"What is it?" he asked.

Shaniqua looked nervous. "He's coming back."

***

The feeling in the pit of Corey's stomach grew worse the further he drove. What in the hell was Regina doing out here with a bunch of farms?

Her location was over an hour away. At first, he thought that he might have been scammed by the app creators because surely she couldn't be all the way out here, but another part of him told him to keep going.

Maybe there was another city on the other side of this rural area.

Part of him hoped there was, but another part hoped there wasn't.

Either way, he hoped it wasn't what he thought, and that Regina would have the perfect explanation for being all the way out here, like she always did.

"Come on baby," he whispered. "Don't let me down."

***

Reggie returned to the building with a smirk on his face.

Shaniqua fought back her expression of disgust. "You know, you didn't have to do that," she said.

Reggie's tone was cool, like this was something he did every day. "What? Kill her? Shit, she was a loose end. We couldn't have her lingering around, getting us caught up in some bullshit."

Shaniqua opened her mouth to protest but decided that she had better play it safe with Reggie. If he killed a girl he grew up with just that easily, then Junior was right. She had no real leg to stand on with him.

Reggie sat on an overturned wooden trunk while Shaniqua sat on a bale of hay. She wanted to help Junior get out of here, but she was scared shitless. She couldn't get the images out of her mind of what Reggie had done to Regina.

Finally, she pulled a plan out of her ass. "Hey, are you hungry?" she asked. "I could go get us some food."

Reggie thought about it for a second. "I suppose that's cool. I could stay here and watch Junior. My ribs are touching like a motherfucker, too. You must have heard my stomach growling. There's a restaurant like fifteen minutes up the highway. It's rundown, but they have good food."

Shaniqua almost opened her mouth to ask Reggie how he knew about the restaurant, but she decided it didn't matter. She needed to get the hell away from him and contact the police. The man had just killed a woman right in front of her. No way was Shaniqua about to be next.

"Okay, cool. I'll go." Shaniqua played it cool, standing up off the bale of hay like she was in no rush to leave. "What do you want?" she added a bored sigh after she spoke for good measure.

Reggie reached into his back pocket for his wallet, opening it and pulling out a twenty. "Their food is really cheap. Maybe just a burger or something for me, then you can get what you want with the rest."

Shaniqua took the twenty, urging herself not to look too eager. She could not betray her emotions at this time. If she did, she was going to end up on top of Regina in that hole Reggie dug. "Cool, let me get the keys."

Reggie put his wallet back in the first pocket, then reached in his other back pocket for the car keys.

Shaniqua's heart was racing a mile a minute. Right before the keys touched her hand, they heard a vehicle swerve off the side of the road, then a car door slam.

Reggie's head whipped toward the main door of the building.

"What the hell?"

Chapter 22

This was some bullshit, Corey could tell. He tried to hold out hope that his woman was really down for him, but when he saw Regina's car carelessly parked across the grass like he wasn't shit, Corey knew he had gotten played, yet again. Then he caught himself. He was jumping to conclusions, something he sometimes did when he was anxious. This whole situation was bothersome for him. He didn't like being in the middle of drama between his favorite cousin and his girlfriend. It was too stressful.

Then his mind thought of something else. Why the hell would Regina come all the way out to an abandoned building? Was she in some kind of trouble? Corey took a step forward, then heard a male's voice from inside the building. It sounded like he was asking who was outside. Corey's fists balled at his sides as he fumed. His suspicions were confirmed. Regina cheated.

Images of all the times he and Regina had shared flashed through his mind, then dissipated as if they had gone up in flames.

Regina was nothing more than a repeat of Ashley.

His heart hardened. "Fuck both of those bitches!" he spat.

Corey was turning to walk away, but the door to one of the abandoned buildings opened, and a nigga he somewhat recognized walked out with a menacing expression on his face.

Who the fuck is this nigga? Corey thought. *And why meet Regina in a barn? Is he homeless or something?*

Corey stepped closer, trying to remember where he knew this dude from, when all of a sudden, the man whipped out a gun.

Immediately, Corey put his hands up. "Wait!"

***

Reggie was pissed as a motherfucker. What should have been a simple, easy transaction was turning into a real problem.

How the fuck did Regina's man find out about this place? Did she tell him she was coming? Reggie looked back at the barn.

Maybe Shaniqua had told. Reggie's expression darkened as he thought of what he would do to her if he found out she crossed him.

Reggie was ready to give Shaniqua the world, until it became possible that she was a snake.

"Come on, man. Don't shoot me," Corey, Regina's bitch ass man, pleaded.

Reggie was disgusted. It was difficult for him to end Regina, given their history, but Reggie almost couldn't wait to get rid of this nigga.

"Sorry, pretty boy," Reggie said, his gun still trained on Corey. His punk ass didn't even try to rush him or anything when he had turned away for that brief moment. "You fucked with the wrong one."

***

"Shit!" Shaniqua's mind was frantic as she saw Reggie pull out the gun. He was really about to kill another person right in front of her. She was nowhere near over what he'd just done to Regina.

Her eyes shot back and forth between Junior on the floor and Reggie outside. She had to do something. She had to think quickly.

"Shaniqua, come on!" Junior pleaded with his life, a tear streaming down each cheek. "Please."

Shaniqua was ready to move. If either of them wanted to get out of this situation alive, she had to break Junior out of that rope. Her eyes were frantic as they searched the barn for something sharp. Then she thought that she could just try to untie it. Reggie tied the rope pretty tightly. Hopefully it wouldn't be too difficult for Shaniqua to undo what he had done.

"Turn around," Shaniqua urged as she gestured. "We gotta move quick!"

Just as Junior was turning his body so Shaniqua could untie the rope, a shot rang out.

***

Everything felt like it happened in slow motion. One second, Corey was a badass, coming to this spot to fight for his woman.

Now, he had a gun trained on him, and his rival had just pulled the trigger.

All Corey remembered seeing was Reggie's wrist flinch as the gun went off, sending a bullet to the middle of his chest.

His body flopped back in slow motion.

Corey felt himself hitting the ground.

He heard footsteps as Reggie walked closer, then his eyes rolled back as Reggie stepped into his line of vision.

"Told you it wasn't a game," Reggie whispered.

Chapter 23

Shaniqua was at her wits end, but she didn't know what to do. After shooting Corey in the chest, Reggie stared at the man lying on the ground, his blood pooling around him with a smirk on his face.

Shaniqua ran over, due to a weirdly misguided reflex, and saw it. She wished her body had not worked that way. Now, she couldn't un-see the scene herself. Corey lying in a pool of blood. Innocent Corey. Reggie told her all about him.

Reggie turned to her with that cold, black stare.

"Watch Junior," was all he said before hoisting Corey over his shoulders as he had done Regina.

Watching Reggie carry another grown man like he was a ragdoll was too much for Shaniqua. She raced over to the bale of hay that she had previously been sitting on and retched out all of her insides in one motion.

Junior was pleading for her to help him, but his voice was so far away.

Junior didn't understand. He didn't see what Shaniqua had just saw. Shaniqua and Junior were both going to die at the hands of Reggie, and it was no fault but their own for associating with him. Whatever Junior had done, it must have been bad.

Shaniqua was heaving, she was so shaken by the day's events. She knew she couldn't fall apart if she had any hope whatsoever of staying alive. She had to find the resolve within herself to fight. Fight for her life, and Junior's, if it was possible.

She pulled herself together, straightening up both physically and mentally, then turned to face Junior to try to help him once again to get out of those ropes.

Before she could take a step toward him, Reggie came in the side door she had originally looked out of when he was throwing Regina's body in the hole out back.

Shaniqua reasoned that he must have just done the same with Corey's.

His wifebeater was drenched in blood, but his jeans were remarkably clean.

Reggie must have noticed Shaniqua staring because he looked down at his shirt. "Fuck! That nigga fucked up my shit!" he growled.

Then he grinned. "Good thing I made provisions for this sort of thing."

"Provisions?" Shaniqua couldn't help but ask. Why was Reggie always going on about some damn provisions he had made?

Junior was on the ground, mumbling and praying.

Both Reggie and Shaniqua were ignoring him at the moment.

Reggie stared at Shaniqua with a cool gaze. "I planned and prepared. I'm a thorough ass nigga. A nigga you would have had, by the way," he said, grabbing his crotch and pointing at her, "if I didn't just come to the realization that you were a fucking snake."

Shaniqua would have been disgusted at Reggie grabbing his crotch like that, like she was a piece of meat or something, if there wasn't a more pressing matter to discuss.

"What do you mean, a snake?" she asked. *No!* her mind screamed. This couldn't be happening. There was no way Reggie was about to kill her now, after everything she had just seen.

She didn't even get a chance to fight for herself. A chance to try to escape.

Reggie chuckled, switching from a cool to a menacing gaze. "I was thinking out there," he pointed, "how the fuck did both Regina and Corey show up within an hour of each other? How did either of them even know about this place?"

He pulled out his gun from his waist again, and Shaniqua's breath quickened.

The words tumbled out of her mouth. "I texted Regina," she started, but Reggie cut her off, raising the gun at Shaniqua's face.

"Shut the FUCK UP!" he screamed.

Shit! her mind screamed.

Junior was wriggling around in the corner, but Reggie didn't seem to notice. Shaniqua wasn't saying shit about it. If she had to die, at least Junior might have a chance.

Reggie continued. "You texted Regina, and you texted that nigga Corey, too. Admit it."

Shaniqua shook her head with force. "No, I didn't. I swear. I only texted Regina, and only because I thought she could help us with the plan." She had lied her ass off about that last part, but if Reggie would take it, it would save her.

Reggie looked like he was considering what she said.

He believes me? Shaniqua's mind said. *Maybe he did like me, after all. If he's willing to actually consider my word when he was just doubting me.*

Reggie's next statement confirmed her suspicions. "I really don't want to kill you, baby girl, but I need to know I can trust you. Give me your phone."

Shaniqua didn't want to at all, but she immediately obeyed, whipping the phone out and handing it to Reggie.

His features softened as he scrolled through her texts. He looked back up at her and nodded, lowering the pointed gun from her face that he had held in his other hand while he was scrolling.

"You told me the truth," he said, nodding again. "The only texts in there are to Regina, Marlena, and me."

Shaniqua nodded, too, playing along. "I would never betray you." She swallowed.

Chapter 24

Shaniqua would never know how elated Reggie was that she had told him the truth. The first female he felt he could truly trust. Not Momma. Not Marlena. Not Regina. *Shaniqua.*

He knew they were a match made in heaven. *Or hell,* his mind said. He smirked at his demented little joke. He decided he'd keep that one to himself. Shaniqua probably wouldn't understand.

He licked his lips while his heart fluttered. He wanted to take her ass down, right then and there, and even in front of Junior, if need be, but he had to keep his head in the game. If Reggie was honest with himself, he had been curious about exploring Shaniqua's body ever since they first met. Ever since that day they saw each other outside that salon.

She was looking good enough to eat then, just like she was right now, and Reggie was starving.

More time for that later, he reminded himself. He had already taken the gun off her, which caused her to calm. He returned it to his waist, which allowed her to breathe even more freely.

"Here's what we're gonna do," he said. "I'm gonna go to the whip and change my shirt. You watch Junior for me."

Shaniqua's eyes shifted. "I can go get the shirt for you. Just give me the keys."

Something about her eyes gave Reggie pause. She was acting too eager. *Is she really down for me?* was his immediate question.

Then he stopped himself. No, he wasn't going to kill her. Shaniqua was trustworthy. His baby would never betray him. She had just said so.

Still, until he could one hundred percent trust her, he decided to meet her halfway about her request.

He pulled his keys out his back pocket and clicked the fob. They had driven his car to this location, and Shaniqua's car was stashed away somewhere safe, in case they needed it to run from the cops or some shit.

Reggie smiled at his baby. "You can go ahead and get the shirt. It's in the back seat."

***

Shaniqua fought with all her might to hide her disappointment as she walked toward the back seat of Reggie's vehicle, which was parked out back behind the building they were located at. Reggie had her move it to the back after he pulled Junior out of the trunk and dumped him on the floor before proceeding to beat his ass.

She wished she had just driven off then and left the men to their own devices. Why hadn't she? What made her stay? She had the keys, she had his car, she had her phone, and there wouldn't have been shit Reggie could do about it. She could have called the police, or not. She could have floored it home, moved to another town, changed her identity... yet, here she was. Stuck. Defenseless. With a deranged, gun-wielding murderer holding her at bay.

She shook her head and tried to think of a plan as she opened the rear passenger's side door and saw the package of crisp white wifebeaters in the back seat, as Reggie had said. It almost made her want to gag again. Reggie had really planned out this entire thing, and for what? What the hell had Junior done that was so bad?

She contemplated asking but didn't know if that would be pushing it.

It could buy you more time, her mind said. *If he's starting to trust you again, maybe playing on his heart strings will put the icing on the cake.*

"STOP fucking moving!" she heard Reggie scream from the inside of the building, snapping her out of her thoughts.

Her heart raced as she quickly grabbed the package of wifebeaters so she wouldn't upset him again.

She closed the car door and whipped around to go back inside, just to hear another gunshot.

Chapter 25

Junior thought he was a dead man, but just as before, Reggie was only fucking with him. He had gotten fed up with trying to wait on Shaniqua to help him and tried to make some real leeway with breaking that damn rope while Reggie was staring at Shaniqua through the side door, but Reggie had turned back and saw his arms moving.

Reggie had immediately stalked over, screaming on him, but Junior was pissed.

They got into a little spat, and Junior told Reggie to untie him so they could fight like men, or just to go ahead and shoot him.

In his mind, it was no time to be a bitch. It was time to man up and fight for his life and Marlena's.

Reggie shot the bullet near his head to scare him, and it worked.

Junior never felt more broken in his life.

This entire time, in between trying to escape little by little and hearing all of Shaniqua and Reggie's bullshit, Junior had been thinking of his baby. How betrayed she must have felt when Reggie and Shaniqua schemed to make it seem like he was cheating.

And it was nobody's fault but Junior's own if Marlena believed them, since he had cheated on her once before.

It was a stupid decision, and it almost cost him the love of his life. He hadn't realized at that point in their relationship that he loved Marlena, though. He suspected that part of the reason he cheated in the first place was because he was afraid. He had never felt the chemistry had with Marlena with another woman.

When he got that other girl pregnant, he never forgot the look on Marlena's face. She'd told him she hated him and broke things off immediately.

Then it was Junior's turn to be devastated. He'd played females before, though he'd never gotten anyone pregnant.

Once Marlena said she was done with him, a piece of him felt like it was irreplaceably lost. Like he needed to get it back to make his life complete.

He felt like he was going crazy. He barely ate or slept. He dreamed and thought about her incessantly. Everything about Marlena, he remembered. Every detail, every fragment. Her smile. The dimple on her left cheek. The way her eyes lit up when he pulled up to see her or take her out on a date.

The sound of her voice on the phone when she lied and told him she wasn't falling asleep, only because she wanted to keep hearing his voice a little longer.

He hadn't realized he stayed on the phone all those times because he wanted to hear her voice, too. And she had broken up with him. And it was his fault. And it hurt.

He cried over a woman for the first time in his life, then he begged to get her back. He vowed he would never do it again. He would never betray her, and to this point, he'd kept his promise.

At first, Junior thought Marlena would never forgive him. She rejected every call, then blocked him. He sent her money through her payment app. She declined it.

He sent flowers to her job. She drove by his house in the middle of the night and hurled them at his bedroom window.

He wrote her love letters, and she ripped them to shreds and stuffed the pieces into his mailbox when he wasn't home.

The one thing that made her give him another chance was when he got down on his knees in the pouring down rain while she was on a date with another nigga.

He didn't give a fuck about pride or nothing like that.

Marlena surprisingly accepted his apology then, to the chagrin of the other dude.

Junior had been on the straight and narrow since then, even when he met Shaniqua. As time had gone by since Marlena took him back, he realized he was ready.

Ready to move forward and make Marlena his wife.

No other woman could touch her warm caress or the softness of her skin. Her words of encouragement or the way she made him feel like a man.

He wanted to continue to be her man, but more than that, he wanted to be the other half of her soul, for life. He had already bought the ring and planned the perfect proposal, to which Marlena had said yes.

Here he was, barely a week later, lying on the floor of an abandoned building, preparing to die.

Hell no, he told himself, *I ain't going out like that.*

Chapter 26

Shaniqua raced back into the building, thinking that Reggie had killed Junior. To her surprise and disgust, however, he had only played another one of his mind games.

"There you go, bitching back up!" Reggie barked. "I thought you said you wanted to fight like a man."

Shaniqua put two and two together and figured that Junior and Reggie must have gotten into some kind of disagreement, and as a result, Reggie shot at Junior.

"Huh, pussy?" Reggie said, walking over and kicking Junior in the ribs. "I can't hear you. Fight me like a man. Fight like you said." He kicked him again.

If Reggie didn't stop, he was going to kill Junior by beating him. He had already beaten him badly when they first got here.

Junior spit out blood.

Shaniqua had to think quick. "Hey, Reggie," she started, trying her best to sound unbothered about the pain that was being inflicted on Junior, "what are we going to do with Corey and Regina's cars? We wouldn't want the cops riding by and getting suspicious."

Reggie finally took his attention off beating Junior.

Thank God, Shaniqua thought.

"You're right," he said. He was silent for a moment, looking at the ground, then he returned her gaze. "We still got their keys. We could move them to the back."

Shaniqua waited a beat like she was thinking about it, then shook her head. "That's too risky. What if they still see them? One car is fine, but three? They might see that from the road."

Once Shaniqua said that Reggie looked like he was getting antsy. That was exactly what Shaniqua wanted. For Reggie to see a weakness in his plan and turn to her for guidance as a result of trust. Once that happened, she was getting those keys, riding the hell out of here, and going straight to the cops. If Reggie wanted to take her on a high-speed chase, so be it. That would make it all the easier to alert the cops and save Junior.

Hopefully.

Shaniqua felt herself getting excited, but her hopes were dashed with Reggie's next words.

His expression brightened. "Shaniqua, you a down ass bitch, you know that? Thank you, baby. I got an idea. Let me make a call."

***

While Reggie stepped away from them, still keeping his eyes on them during his phone call, Shaniqua felt herself becoming more pissed.

Every damn plan she came up with, Reggie hurled it to the ground. To be dumb as hell, he sure was smart at all the wrong moments, and for all the wrong reasons.

"What the hell did you even do to him?" she spat at Junior, breaking character and not giving a fuck if Reggie heard her.

She didn't dare glance back at him on the phone, however. She was still scared of him, pissed or not.

"He already said it," Junior replied. "I stole Marlena from him."

Shaniqua stared at Junior as if he had four heads. "You're serious? That was it?" she said that part in a lower voice since her fear of Reggie was back on the uprise now that his phone conversation seemed like it was ending.

Junior nodded. "That was it."

Shaniqua couldn't believe this shit. She had gotten herself wrapped up in all of this over a silly ass game of catfish? When Junior and Reggie argued earlier about Junior catfishing Marlena to steal her from Reggie, Shaniqua thought there was more to the story. Now that she knew there wasn't, she realized Reggie was truly insane.

They had to stop him.

Her thoughts were interrupted, yet again, as Reggie loudly clapped his hands, walking toward them again.

"Good news, ladies and gents!" he announced. "I got a tow guy on the way to get rid of these cars." He turned to Shaniqua. "After that, we're about to get this shit poppin' for real."

Usually, that dark look Reggie gave her scared Shaniqua shitless, but this time, she felt a little pushback.

Yeah, we gonna get it poppin', alright. Just not the way you think.

Chapter 27

Reggie felt like he was on top of the world. He was about to rid his life of all the snakes who betrayed him and ride off in the sunset with his new bitch, hopefully to a new life.

He knew he would have to leave town permanently after all these bodies.

There was no way the police wouldn't patch together what happened. Regina and Corey had probably left all kinds of evidence behind, not to mention whatever Junior and Marlena would leave.

Reggie wasn't worried, though. No one had ever even questioned him about the other bodies he dropped.

He was good.

He had over twenty racks saved. He figured that was enough money to move to Mexico to start, then he had some cousins in Jamaica. They had been trying to get him in the game out there for a while. Reggie visited Jamaica a few times in his youth and loved it, both the good sides and the dark sides.

The dark sides were where he would likely end up when he moved there with Shaniqua, though.

He glanced at her and envisioned her body in a bikini. His mouth watered. Hell yeah, that would be a sight to see.

Then he snapped out of it. He had to keep his head in the game.

Reggie contemplated for a few minutes whether he should tell any of the current dudes he ran with that he was leaving. He shook his head. Naw, it was too risky, and besides, after today was over, he would have killed his two oldest friends. He didn't think he could stomach many more.

He would just dip out and catch up with them in a few years maybe. They would get over his absence. He'd only been given four corners to run by Bankz, anyway.

Bankz was one of the street generals of the M4FYA gang that Reggie had joined a few years ago. Reggie and Bankz weren't close, but he had served as sort of a mentor to Reggie as he worked his way up the streets. First as a dope boy, then a stick-up kid, then he took out a few of Bankz' enemies, catching those first few bodies, and finally, he graduated to running a few corners of his own.

Reggie was no stranger to the streets. He knew how to survive. He only hoped Shaniqua could become accustomed to the lifestyle they were set to live.

He figured she would, since she had gone along with his plan so easily when he originally made the proposition. Then, she fulfilled her duties with no fuckups. Junior was practically brought to Reggie on a platter.

Yeah, Reggie thought to himself. *She a down ass bitch, alright.*

***

Although Shaniqua was ready to take action against Reggie, she was finding it harder to just make a move. Her mind asked her, *what the hell can you really do to him?* Where would Shaniqua go? She wasn't a fighter, so that was out. Reggie would more than likely rip her to pieces.

There was absolutely nothing she could use as a weapon in this godforsaken building.

Reggie also still had the car keys in his back pocket, along with the gun in his waistband.

What the hell could Shaniqua do?

She thought to distract him, but before she could open her mouth, she heard the tow truck pulling up.

Unbelievable.

That's the fastest damn tow truck I've ever heard of in my life! The truck showed up in barely thirty minutes.

What kind of people did Reggie really know? Did they get here that fast because they wanted the money? Or did Reggie already have them waiting nearby and was just fucking with her when he said she had given him a good idea?

It seemed that no matter what Shaniqua thought or did, she was always back to square one with Reggie.

The worst part was that time was running out.

Chapter 28

Junior had no idea what the hell Shaniqua's problem was. She had so many opportunities to get out of this building, walking around as freely as she had been, but she'd never taken it.

Now that the tow truck was outside to get Corey and Regina's cars, Junior was ready for action.

His heart broke for Marlena because he knew she would be devastated over her cousin, but in Junior's mind, Corey had some fuck shit with him, too. How the hell did he get caught up in this plan? Corey was working with Reggie behind his back, too?

And what the hell was wrong with Regina? What had Junior ever done to her to make her turn on him to try to kill him?

If anything, Junior thought he and Regina were cooler than Regina and Reggie had been. Junior stayed working at the factory long after Reggie left to run the streets. They had worked the same station every day together for over a year. What the fuck was wrong with her?

He had no time to think about that. His blade had finally cut his hands free.

He prayed Shaniqua would go outside with Reggie to talk to the tow guy, and if she did, he was cutting his legs free and busting the fuck up out of here.

Reggie turned toward Junior when the tow truck guy backed up at an angle so he could get Regina's car first.

"Sit tight," he said with a smirk, then walked outside. "Watch him," Reggie said to Shaniqua.

Bitch better stay away, Junior thought as he eyed Shaniqua. He hadn't revealed to her that his hands were free because he was hoping she would stop paying attention to him for a second and focus on Reggie. Junior couldn't have her screaming or anything when he was so close to freedom.

When the beeping sound was made outside, signaling that the first car was being loaded onto the truck, Shaniqua finally broke eye contact with Junior and walked toward the door to check on Reggie.

Junior wasted no time.

With a burst of energy, he sprang into action, easily snapping the rest of the rope that was holding his hands, then sitting up to cut his legs free. He aggressively attacked the rope while Shaniqua peeked her head out the door. It took him four swipes and he was done. He jumped to his feet and raced toward the side door just as Shaniqua turned due to hearing his sudden movement.

"Hey!" she said, but Junior was already out the door.

***

"Shit!" Shaniqua said under her breath when Reggie heard her outburst at the sight of Junior breaking free. Now she had no idea what Reggie was going to do.

"What is it?" Reggie said, walking back over. Regina's car had just been lifted onto the truck, and the tow guy was backing up at another angle to get Corey's.

"What is it?" Reggie repeated, walking toward Shaniqua. She didn't know how to answer. What would Reggie do to her?

He pushed past her and saw that Junior was gone. "You let him out?"

"No! He broke free, I swear..." Before Shaniqua finished her sentence, Reggie smacked her so hard she fell to the ground.

The tow guy was preparing Corey's car to be lifted onto his truck behind Regina's. He heard Reggie hit Shaniqua and walked over.

Shaniqua stayed on the ground, whimpering and praying that he would try to help her.

"What's going on, man?" the tow guy asked, but his voice sounded familiar.

No! Shaniqua's mind screamed. This could not be happening. It couldn't be him.

"Watch this bitch for me," Reggie spat.

Shaniqua turned to look, and her worst fears were confirmed. The tow guy just so happened to be the last man she had schemed on. *Rell.* The one who sent her the death threats. Rell's eyes hardened when he recognized her.

He pulled a gun out from the back of his waist and pointed it at Shaniqua. "Go head, Reg," he said. "Take care of your business."

Chapter 29

Junior had never run so fast in his entire life. He felt like a track star as he zig-zagged through the woods, his body hurting like hell, but he had to put distance between him and Reggie, who he heard shouting at him from a distance.

A bullet whizzed past his ear and broke off some of the bark from a tree ahead of him. Junior was sick of being shot at, but he could not die now.

You gotta push, his mind told him. He didn't dare look back to see how close or far Reggie was to him. He hoped to God that the trees would provide a hiding place.

"Shit!" he heard somewhere behind him at a near distance, then it sounded like Reggie had tripped and fallen.

Still, Junior didn't look back. He had to get to Marlena. He ran through swampy looking waters, drenching his pants almost up to the waist, but he kept on going.

He didn't hear Reggie behind him, but he kept on going.

His lungs felt like they were giving out on him, but he kept on going.

Finally, not having any more wind left, he collapsed to the ground, breathing and crying at the same time, praying that he wouldn't open his eyes just to see a bullet race to his head.

He opened his eyes, and Reggie was nowhere to be found.

From the sounds of the cars zipping by him however, he was near a highway. He had to get back to Marlena.

***

This could not be life. Shaniqua looked up at Rell, then slowly rose to her feet. "What are you going to do, huh?" she asked. "You gonna shoot me?"

Rell chuckled, looking disgusted, but maniacal at the same time. Shaniqua could tell he wanted to do far more than shoot her. He wanted to destroy her. "Bitch nigga, I should. I can't believe you did some shit like that to me."

"Should have checked my credentials," Shaniqua said. It was a stupid ass comment, especially seeing that she had a gun pointed at her head, but Shaniqua had long stopped being afraid of bullies.

Reggie, she was afraid of because he was a stone-cold murderer, but Rell was just a man who prided himself on fucking with people he thought were weaker than him.

Shaniqua could tell the difference because she had lived it.

In all her life, she lived as a young girl in a boy's body. She faced various kinds of torture. All from boys who grew up to be men like Rell.

Hell no, she wasn't scared. If she died at the hands of Rell, she would go out swinging.

***

Reggie was pissed as fuck. Junior had gotten away, and now his jeans were ripped. "I'm-a fucking kill that nigga, I swear!" he said. He went back to the building, formulating a new plan on the way.

He would get Junior, he told himself. He knew just what to do to make him come back running.

***

Junior found himself on the highway, holding his hand out and trying to hitchhike, but no one was stopping for him. He didn't really know where he was, but he imagined he couldn't be that far from home seeing that Regina and Corey had gotten to the buildings in such close timing as each other. It hadn't taken the tow guy that long, either. If the tow guy lived in town like Corey and Regina did, Junior didn't have that far to go. He just needed a ride.

Finally, a minivan pulled over to the side of the road.

"Thank God," Junior said, racing over.

The older lady and her husband rolled down the passenger side window of their car. "Young man, are you lost?" the older man asked.

Junior nodded eagerly. "Yes, Sir. I'm stranded." He told them the name of his hometown, and the wife's eyes lit up. "Oh, that's marvelous, dear! We can drop you off at the bus station."

Junior was disappointed at the fact that they wouldn't just bring him home, especially seeing that he didn't have any money on him to take the bus, but he was grateful for the ride. He got in the back seat.

"Thank you," he said, then strapped on his seatbelt.

Chapter 30

Rell's eyes lit up when he saw Shaniqua wasn't scared of him. Shaniqua wasn't sure if that was a good or bad thing. He lowered his gun with a chuckle.

Good thing, Shaniqua thought.

"Oh, so you want to act like a man now?" Rell said, cracking his neck. "Let's see if you can fight like one."

Shaniqua didn't flinch. She might not be able to take him, but she would damn sure fight like she could. "Let's go, pussy," she said, lowering her voice a few octaves to its true tone. She had taken hormone therapy treatments to try to change her voice when she transitioned a few years ago, but the therapy hadn't changed her tone completely. The doctors had told her it wouldn't, but she held out hope anyhow. In conjunction with the hormone therapy, she sought out a voice coach to help her get her voice to a female-sounding octave. Thankfully, that plan worked.

Rell's face scrunched up when he heard her words, then he swung.

Shaniqua blocked his punch easily, though his fist had certainly hurt her forearm. The satisfaction from seeing him pissed at the prospect of losing the fight, however, was worth the pain.

"Bitch!" Rell spat on the ground, then swung again.

Shaniqua ducked this time, almost a millisecond too late.

She was about to say something else when Rell caught her off guard and rammed his body into hers, knocking her to the ground.

"What, you want a round two?" she sneered, then she kneed him in the balls.

"Fucking bitch!" Rell grunted and wrenched her arms down as she tried to swing up at him. She struggled against him, but Reggie banged into the building before anything else could happen.

"Fuck you doing, nigga?" Reggie asked, taking in the scene before him.

From the outside eye, it looked more like Rell was trying to rape Shaniqua than what it really was.

Rell immediately got up, and Shaniqua was thankful. Rell was sort of on the stockier side, so his weight was starting to crush her.

"It's nothing, man. I was just..." Rell stammered.

Reggie smirked and cut him off. "Nigga, how dare you try to sample my shit before I do?"

Rell wasn't sure how to take Reggie's words, Shaniqua could tell. As she got up, she realized she wasn't sure how to take them, either. She hoped this situation was not about to turn into some further bullshit. One man, she could fight off, but two?

"Go on, nigga," Reggie said. "I gotta get these cars out the way."

"No doubt," Rell said, and he hurried to get Corey's car onto his truck, then drove off without another word.

Shaniqua didn't know how to feel. Not a cop or car or anyone who could help had driven by all day. Was this place really that inconspicuous? What happened with Junior? Shaniqua thought she had heard a gunshot earlier, but she was too preoccupied with settling the score with Rell to really question it.

She wasn't sure if Junior was dead or alive. All she knew was that if she didn't find a way out, she was next.

***

The elderly couple dropped Junior off at the bus station as promised. He knew he was looking crazy as hell with a dirty undershirt and ripped and muddied jeans, not to mention the smell of piss that was emanating from them, but he had to get to Marlena. He'd ditched his regular t-shirt before hitting the highway because he didn't want people questioning why he had blood on him.

Now, he had to walk home looking crazy and hope he got there before Reggie decided to do anything further.

***

Reggie pulled out Shaniqua's phone from his back pocket. "Junior got away," he informed her. "So now we gotta move forward with plan B."

"What's plan B?" Shaniqua asked, looking nervous.

He handed her the phone. "Call Marlena."

Chapter 31

Marlena decided she had enough. She'd been sitting in that same spot in the kitchen off and on for hours. She'd gone to the package store to get some Henny, drank about half the bottle, smoked some weed, and yet, nothing could take her mind off Junior.

Half of her wanted to just let Shaniqua and whoever she was working with keep him.

The other half wanted to save her man.

"Am I really this weak? This dumb? Why save a nigga that clearly cheated?" Marlena had had plenty of boyfriends in her life due to always being the pretty, popular girl, but unfortunately, being pretty and popular couldn't make a nigga treat her right. Before Reggie and Junior both cheated, she had countless other cheating boyfriends. Well, not countless, because she was far from a hoe, but she'd been through enough to say Junior was her last straw before she decided to just be single for a while.

She shook her head. Marlena could not believe after everything she had gone through with Junior, after he hunted her down in the pouring rain and got down on his knees to beg her to take him back, that he was still an ain't-shit nigga who wasn't worth the trouble.

But what if they didn't have sex, though? her mind asked.

"It doesn't fucking matter!" she spat. "He still wanted to. He went to the bitches' house at three in the morning. What else could it be for, Mar?"

Still, she couldn't stop looking at that photo of her man bound and gagged, and Shaniqua with that, *yeah, I got him bitch* look on her face. Who in the fuck did Shaniqua think she was?

Marlena thought that she and Shaniqua were cool, especially since they'd gotten so close so quickly. Shaniqua informed her that she was the only person she'd ever been able to tell right off the bat that she'd been born a male.

Marlena kept her secret and encouraged her, just like a good friend would.

"And this is how the bitch repays me," Marlena said to herself. "By literally stealing my goddamn man."

Granted, Marlena asked Shaniqua to see if Junior would try to talk to her, but still. She truly hoped Junior wouldn't bite the bait. He told her he loved her, and she believed him because she loved him.

He acted like he was so faithful after she'd found out about his first cheating incident. He showed her his phone and everything...

"His phone!" Marlena screamed suddenly. Her mind thought back. When was the last time Junior showed her his phone? She remembered going through it the night he proposed after they had spent hours making blissful love.

She had to be sure then, and she thought everything was good.

"But the reason I thought everything was good was because I didn't see shit in there."

That's right. You didn't see shit in there, her mind said.

"But wait..." Marlena started piecing things together. "If I didn't see shit in Junior's phone a week ago, how the hell has he been flirting with Shaniqua for weeks? Where were the messages? Did he delete them? Did he have another phone?"

All these questions were too much, and Marlena became pissed, yet filled with resolve all over again. She was calling that fucking number, and she and Shaniqua were going to have a face-to-face meeting.

She grabbed the phone, prepared to press 1, then the green button as instructed, but before she could even swipe the screen, the phone rang.

Marlena scrunched up her face in confusion, then answered.

"Hello?"

Chapter 32

When Reggie held out Shaniqua's phone and told her to call Marlena, Shaniqua's mind immediately started racing. Why couldn't Reggie just leave well enough alone? He'd already beaten Junior's ass multiple times and scared him half to death. Judging from the way he hightailed it out of the building, Shaniqua was sure Junior was all set with ever fucking with Reggie again. Why still try to go through with the plan? Especially over something so stupid.

All this over a damn catfish? she thought, but then she felt like a complete hypocrite. She had catfished the hell out of Rell and the two other men before him, then laughed all the way to the bank when they decided they would rather pay her two thousand dollars each out of their hard-earned money than be outed for sleeping with a man.

For the men that Shaniqua played, it was less about having their feelings hurt or feeling embarrassed, and it was more about their dignity and self-respect. In their eyes, and probably most of society's, Shaniqua had violated them to the highest degree possible. Even though they could probably tell their friends until they were blue in the face that they had no idea she was born a male, no one would believe them, and for their supposed indiscretion, they would be ostracized, like Shaniqua had been all her life.

The fact that these men would only get a glimpse of something she had dealt with her entire life was part of the reason Shaniqua relished in the idea of outing them even after they paid the money. Of course, she hadn't done it and never would because even though part of her still hated herself, she loved the fact that she was still breathing.

She still had hopes, dreams, and aspirations buried underneath her pain.

Being part of Reggie's evil scheme, however, Shaniqua realized that there was a very real chance that her hopes, dreams, and aspirations would never be realized. Instead, she'd be dead. Thrown in a miserable hole on top of the dead man and woman who were already laying there.

Her mind went, once again, to Regina and Corey, and the fate they suffered. Corey was the only truly innocent one in all this. Regina previously revealed that she lied to him about Marlena to get him on board. Corey was acting on misguided love for his girlfriend by betraying his cousin, along with his belief that he was honestly doing Marlena a favor. Corey was led to believe that Junior really was cheating on Marlena with her.

Then, he had come here, likely to fight Reggie and get his woman back, only to get hit with a bullet to the chest and lose his life. It was pitiful. Pathetic.

It was horrible, but Corey's fate only made Shaniqua feel sorrier for herself.

Is this how my story really ends? she asked herself, but she didn't get much of a chance to ponder it longer. Reggie swiped his hand in front of her face, his growing impatience evident in his features.

"Come on, ma," he growled. "I don't have all day."

Reluctantly, and praying Marlena would not answer and that Junior had somehow miraculously gotten to her already to let her know the deal, Shaniqua called the burner phone that Reggie bought from the corner store.

Marlena answered, and Shaniqua fixed her face before responding. She had to put on the performance of a lifetime to convince Reggie once again she wasn't a snake. In return, however, she would be endangering the life of the one woman she ever could have called a true friend.

Chapter 33

When Marlena answered the phone and heard Shaniqua's voice on the other end, she could not believe her fucking audacity. "Bitch, who the fuck do you think you are?" Marlena boomed, letting Shaniqua know through her tone that no games were being played today, and that Shaniqua better be ready to catch these hands if she really wanted to face her.

"I'm the bitch who kidnapped your man," Shaniqua countered, letting Marlena know that she gave not one fuck about the bass in Marlena's voice.

Marlena pulled the phone away from her ear, stared at it, then put it back to her ear again. "Okay, I see what type of time you're on. I gave you a few hours to settle yourself and return my man back, but now I see you think I'm the one you can play with. You about to learn a serious lesson, you weird ass bitch."

"Weird ass bitch?" Shaniqua said with a chuckle. "Ain't that the pot calling the kettle black? How am I the weird ass bitch when you were the one in my ear crying about how you hoped your man wasn't cheating on you and hitting my line every fucking day to see if he gave in to me? Bitch, if I can steal your man that easily, your weak ass pussy must not have been shit. Better learn how to keep him next time."

Marlena was so heated at those words she didn't know what to say next. A large part of her was cut to the heart by Shaniqua's words because that was one of the things Marlena worried about with Junior. Was she bad in bed? Was her cooking not good enough? What was it that made him trample on her heart in the way that he had?

Even though Marlena had always been the pretty, popular girl, a part of her still always second-guessed herself. She walked around with cockiness and confidence and even often genuinely felt that way, but the fact that she went through failed relationship after failed relationship made her think maybe she wasn't as great as she thought she was. She scrolled through social media all the time and saw all those happy couples. She was nearing thirty years old, and all the girls she grew up with were married with children. Why not Marlena? What did they have that she didn't have? What made them good enough to be eligible for a good man, while Marlena seemed to be lacking?

When she met Junior, Marlena honestly thought her wait was over. She took her time and got to know him. She allowed herself to be friends with him first before anything sexual happened. She tried her best to support and love him and keep her attitude in check, and still... nothing. Still, he cheated. Still, he came to her one day with tears in his eyes telling her that he got a whole other bitch pregnant as a result of a *mistake*.

Mistake, Marlena's ass. She'd written him off that day and vowed she would never let another man play her for a fool.

As the days and weeks began to unfold, however, her mind began to eat at her. Little things would come to her, like Junior's smile. His little crooked tooth that stole her heart. The way he held her. The way he stayed up with her all night the day her grandfather died. How he held her hand at the funeral and stood by her like a rock.

She really thought they were in love. She really thought Junior was the one for her.

When they laid up with each other at night, their heartbeats matched. Junior felt safe. He felt like home. How could it all be a lie?

Marlena blinked back her tears and forced herself back into the conversation with Shaniqua. No way in hell was she letting this bitch think she had the upper hand. Yes, Marlena had gotten played yet again, and yes, her heart was broken, but there was one thing Marlena would never let another bitch or a nigga take from her: her dignity or her pride. Fuck that shit.

"Bitch, you flapping your gums over there mighty heavy, but I have yet to be sent the addy. You taking me on a wild ass goose chase when we could have been thrown those hands. Wassup? Stop playing. If you really about that life, send me the addy, and I'll show your former-man ass these hands."

"Say less, bitch," was Shaniqua's reply, and a few seconds later, a notification buzzed in Marlena's ear.

It was the address.

The town was one Marlena recognized by name only, since she had never been there, but she would find it, horrible sense of direction and all. That was what the GPS was for.

"See you soon, bitch. Better grease up your face since that's the only shit you got going for you."

Marlena hung up in Shaniqua's face before she had a chance to respond.

Chapter 34

Shaniqua handed the phone back to a grinning Reggie with nothing but hurt in her heart, though she wouldn't dare show it. Her mind was reeling, but at the same time she thanked God Reggie hadn't forced her to put the phone on speaker. She prayed Reggie hadn't heard Marlena's last comment. Judging from how he'd been acting all day, if he found out she was transgender, her life was over. Her mind flashed back to her former friend. She knew Marlena didn't mean the things she said to her, just like Shaniqua hadn't meant the things she said to Marlena.

Although now wasn't the time to get into a deep thought process about why women chose to low blow each other during arguments, especially when they claimed to be the best of friends before the argument, Shaniqua couldn't help but to let her mind go there for a second. Why did she and Marlena feel the need to go as low as they could when insulting one another? Why hit a person where they knew it would hurt if we claimed to value each other? Shaniqua hadn't known Marlena all her life or anything, but over the past few months of getting to know her, she knew Marlena was a genuine person and that she genuinely enjoyed Shaniqua's friendship. Shaniqua genuinely liked Marlena, too.

With the comments they just said to each other, however, a person on the outside would have never known it. If the circumstances were different, Marlena and Shaniqua might have had their fight, then made up later, apologizing for what they said to each other. Would the pain of what was said ever go away, though? Or would they always see each other with a slightly new set of eyes, each woman keeping her guard up just in case the other decided to say something hurtful again?

"What's wrong with you?" Reggie asked, looking at her with concern.

Shaniqua blinked and shook her head. She was surprised that Reggie was showing any form of compassion for her. She guessed it meant he no longer saw her as a snake, and that he must not have heard Marlena's comment. Still, she knew she had to stay on her toes if she wanted to survive this. Reggie might be cool with her now, based on his facial expression and tone of voice, but as she had seen throughout this day, his temper was volatile at best. Yeah, she'd better play her cards close to her vest.

"Nothing," she said. "I'm just still really hungry. We never got our food earlier. When I get hungry, I tend to space out a lot."

Reggie nodded. "Me too. No worries, baby girl. After we kill Marlena and Junior, we will go to one of those all-you-can-eat buffets. We might have to travel a little first, though." He chuckled, and Shaniqua once again had to hold back her disgust.

Dear God, she prayed internally, *please save me from this man. He is crazy!*

"I guess that's cool," she said aloud. "I hope Marlena hurries up. I'm ready to get this over with. Are you killing her as soon as she gets here, or what?"

Shaniqua felt sick to her stomach even saying those words, but she had to play her part.

Reggie looked like he was thinking about it. "I'm not sure," he finally replied. "I was thinking of torturing her a little first, then killing her in front of Junior when he gets here. That sound good?"

Vomit rushed to the top of Shaniqua's throat at those words, but she swallowed it back and nodded. "Yeah, that sounds good," she said. "You have to teach them that they can't fuck with you and get away with it."

Reggie's eyes lit up. "See, Shaniqua? I knew you was a down ass bitch. Me and you about to have some bomb ass babies."

Shaniqua just blinked at that one, then went to go sit on her bale of hay.

Chapter 35

Marlena cussed Shaniqua out to herself the whole way over to the random ass address Shaniqua had sent. "She better not be playing no damn games, either," Marlena said. She was tired of driving around like a puppet on a string, picking up pictures and notes at different locations like they were breadcrumbs or something. Marlena and Shaniqua weren't in high school. They were two grown ass women. If Shaniqua had a problem with Marlena, she should have been said that shit.

The little back and forth they just had was one of the reasons Marlena didn't trust too many females. Yeah, Marlena was considered popular and everything in her younger years, but only a few girls had actually made it to her inner circle, and even those bitches had to be fully vetted on a regular basis.

Her mind went to Junior once again. In between cussing Shaniqua out to herself, Marlena was half-cussing Junior, too. The jury was still out on whether she would do anything to help him. She might just go to this location, beat Shaniqua's ass, then spit in Junior's face for breaking her heart. After that, Marlena would be done with both of them. They could have each other, for all she cared.

So why even travel all the way out here, then? her mind said. *Why not just tell her over the phone that she could have him?*

"Shut up," Marlena said back to her mind.

Then something dawned on Marlena. Where the hell was Corey? She had called and texted him repeatedly after he sent her the screenshots showing that Junior was going to Shaniqua's house, then dropped the bomb that Shaniqua had HIV. Corey had never written her back, and that wasn't like him. Marlena and Corey had been thick as thieves their entire lives. Their family often joked that they might as well call themselves brother and sister rather than cousins because they certainly acted like it. Marlena's heart panged. Outside of Shaniqua, Corey was the only person who truly knew how devastated she would be at Junior's cheating. Corey could also relate to Marlena's situation, seeing that he had struck out with love quite a few times himself.

Corey had broken up with his girlfriend, Ashley, a few months ago, and it sent him into a depression. Then, all of a sudden, he started acting like a new man, like he no longer gave a damn about Ashley. Marlena asked him multiple times what was really going on. How he could act so devastated one week, then act like he never met the girl the very next week? Corey just kept playing it off and saying their relationship wasn't that serious, but Marlena knew better. She knew Corey loved that girl, just like she loved Junior. Ashley had cheated on Corey in the worst way, ironically, with one of his boys, and had gotten an STD.

Marlena froze when she thought of that. *What the hell? Ain't that the exact same thing that just happened with me and Junior?* Now that she thought of it, the parallels were crazy. Ashley fucked one of Corey's boys and got an STD, and Junior was going over Shaniqua's house to fuck, and she had HIV.

"Hmmm..." Marlena said, feeling stupid all of a sudden.

Now that Marlena thought of it like that, this entire situation was random as hell. How did Corey even know Shaniqua had HIV? From what Marlena knew, Corey and Shaniqua didn't talk to each other. They weren't friends like Shaniqua and Marlena were.

The more Marlena thought about it, the less everything that happened today made sense. Thankfully, in about five minutes, she was about to have some answers.

Marlena pulled up to the third abandoned building in a row of three that were spaced apart from each other. Miraculously, her GPS had worked perfectly this time, so she didn't get lost. Marlena chuckled to herself as she got out of the car. Shaniqua lived only about fifteen minutes from her, and her GPS was rerouting like a motherfucker, but navigating to this random ass barn-looking building in the middle of nowhere was a piece of cake.

Marlena walked through the waist high grass when she noticed other vehicles had been here recently. She could see their tracks and where they had driven in. What the hell did Shaniqua really have going on?

Marlena suddenly felt insecure. What if there was a pack of bitches here, waiting to jump her? She hadn't thought about that.

Then she saw what looked like blood in the clearing near the door of the building. *Blood?* The hairs on the back of Marlena's neck stood up. Why was there blood? Had she just made the dumbest decision of her life?

Before she could think further, the door to the building banged open, startling her, and Shaniqua walked out alone with a smirk on her face.

Marlena was about to say something when she felt and heard movement behind her, then the clicking of a gun.

"Don't move if you want to live," a familiar-sounding male voice said.

Marlena held her hands up and fought the urge to turn around.

"Reggie?" she asked. Reggie was Junior's best friend. Those two were thick as thieves, just like Marlena and Corey. What the hell was Reggie doing here, and how did he know Shaniqua? "Reggie," Marlena repeated. "What the hell is going on?"

Chapter 36

Junior was exhausted, but he finally stepped onto him and Marlena's street. He had never felt so happy to be home and alive. He desperately wanted and needed a shower, but first he had to see his baby. He had to make sure she was okay and tell her about everything that transpired today.

As he walked, Junior formulated a plan. Once he spoke to Marlena, they would go straight to the police. Reggie's ass needed to be put under the jail after what he'd done to Regina and Corey. Granted, Regina was a snake who was somehow part of all this. How, Junior didn't know, but at the same time, the girl had grown up with him and Reggie. How could Reggie kill her like that? And Corey. Junior and Corey were cool as fuck.

"Wait a minute. How the hell did Corey know Regina?" Junior stopped in his tracks in the middle of the street. He and Reggie had grown up with Regina, but he could have sworn that Shaniqua mentioned Corey coming to the location because Regina had texted him. How the hell did those two know each other?

This entire situation was bizarre. So many questions, and not enough answers. Junior didn't have time to process all that just yet, though. Right now, he needed to see Marlena's face. He continued walking, then stopped in his tracks once again as he turned the corner to the duplex where he and Marlena lived.

His heart sank. Her car wasn't there.

Tears burned in the back of Junior's eyes as his mind went frantic. Where was she? Had she left him? Did she go try to find him? Did Reggie somehow get her after he escaped?

He didn't even want to enter their apartment now, not knowing what he might find or what condition the place might be in.

"I swear, if he hurt her..." Junior growled. He approached the door, then patted his pockets and realized he didn't have his keys. Reggie had taken everything from him but had somehow missed his blade.

"Dumbass," Junior spat. The blade was what had set him free. He kept it in the small side pocket of his jeans. That was probably why Reggie missed it. His wallet and keys were in the larger main pockets.

"Blade can't do shit now for me, though," he said under his breath, staring at the door. Then he decided to just try the knob.

To his surprise, the door opened. Marlena must have left in haste. He walked inside and saw a half empty bottle of Henny on the kitchen table. The kitchen also smelled like weed. His heart sank again. Marlena didn't even smoke weed. Her mind must have been all over the place as a result of him being kidnapped.

When Junior saw the pictures and notes splayed across the kitchen table near the bottle of Henny, he knew where Marlena was.

Reggie had her. Either he had come and gotten her, or she had gone willingly, likely trying to save him. Either way, there was only one option for Junior.

He had to go back.

His mind began racing again, trying to come up with a new plan now that Marlena was in real danger. He needed to get his car from Shaniqua's house.

"I don't have my keys..." he began, then he remembered that when he first got the car, he was given two sets of keys. Marlena put the extra set somewhere.

"Where did she put them?" he said to himself, going through all the kitchen drawers, then he made his way to him and Marlena's bedroom. There they were, hanging on a key rack on the wall along with an extra apartment key in case either of them lost theirs.

Junior swallowed back his emotions at the thought of his woman possibly being beaten or tortured by Reggie while he was here at their apartment.

He sprang into action, rushing out of the apartment and running toward Shaniqua's house. Long gone was his exhaustion, as well as his thoughts about taking a shower and getting cleaned up. He had to save his baby.

He got to Shaniqua's house about a half hour later, and thankfully, his car was still there. He hopped inside and barely even checked his mirrors before peeling off her street, headed toward those godforsaken buildings.

Chapter 37

Marlena felt like the biggest fool of the century. She had come all the way out here to fight Shaniqua and save Junior, and come to find out, Junior's ass wasn't even here. Instead, it was a demented looking Reggie and Shaniqua.

And now Marlena was duct taped to a damn chair.

She would have tried to fight or run if it wasn't for the gun Reggie had pointed at her head. He instructed her to sit in the wooden chair and for Shaniqua to tape her up. First her wrists, then her midsection to the back of the chair, then each of her ankles to the legs of the chair.

"Is all this necessary?" she asked when Shaniqua was taping her ankles to the chair legs. "I clearly can't move, and even if I could, Reggie has a gun."

Shaniqua hadn't responded to her question, so Marlena looked up at Reggie's sinister ass.

He smirked. "We gotta tie you up since we won't be here long. Me and my baby about to be out this bitch soon as we kill you and Junior."

Marlena's mind immediately went haywire. She didn't know what to ask first. "Your baby?" She looked at Shaniqua, who suddenly appeared as if she'd seen a ghost. Marlena took from that facial expression that Reggie wasn't aware that Shaniqua was transgender. She decided to keep it from him for now, in case she could get Shaniqua to help her. "Why are you killing me and

Junior, Reggie? I thought you and Junior were friends. What the hell is going on here, and what do I have to do with y'all beef, anyway?" Marlena had never been more confused in her life, but Reggie's response only confused her further.

"You betrayed me," was all he said.

"Reggie, how did I betray you? And where is Junior? Y'all sent me on a wild goose chase to come here for him, and I don't see him anywhere. And is Corey a part of this, too? Where is Corey?"

At this point, Marlena was just spouting out questions due to the fact that Reggie was still pointing his gun in her face. She hoped the longer she kept him talking, the more she could somehow convince him and Shaniqua to spare her life. She'd never done a thing to Reggie. What the hell was he on talking about she betrayed him? And Corey helped set her up, too?

"Where is Corey?" she repeated.

"He's dead!" Shaniqua spat, a wild look in her eyes before Reggie could respond.

Marlena's entire body grew hot and cold at those words. She chuckled. "Bullshit. Where is my cousin?" She turned to Reggie. "Where is my cousin, Reggie?"

She noticed that neither of them broke their stares. A horrible feeling began in the pit of her stomach and rose to her throat in a scream. "You killed my cousin? Where is he? Where is Corey!"

Reggie looked like he felt no remorse. "That nigga dead, ma."

Shaniqua jumped in. "Yeah, that's right. Shot him in the chest at point blank range. Him and Regina are both out back, thrown in a hole Reggie dug. You'll be there soon, too. Don't worry. We'll reunite you with your precious cousin."

"Help!" Marlena screamed over and over again when she heard that.

Reggie looked like he'd had enough. "Tape that bitches' mouth or something, damn!" he said to Shaniqua, then walked out the door to the building.

Shaniqua stared at Marlena with tears in her eyes.

Tears? Marlena thought. *Why does she look like she's about to cry?* Shaniqua opened her mouth to say something, but Reggie banged back into the door. Shaniqua quickly taped Marlena's mouth shut, but Marlena noticed her hands were trembling.

The wheels began to turn in Marlena's mind. If she could get Shaniqua to help her, she might be able to break free from Reggie.

The only question left was, where the hell was Junior?

Chapter 38

Shaniqua fought the urge to feel hopeless. She hoped even if Marlena did end up dead, she knew Shaniqua didn't really want to help with it. She didn't want parts in any of this. If she had a magic wand and could erase the past few months, hell, the past few years, she would do it in a heartbeat. At this point, Shaniqua would erase her entire existence.

She liked being a schemer and a player during the brief time she was making money, but she never wanted to be a murderer.

I gotta find a way away from this man. She stared back and forth between Marlena and Reggie.

***

Reggie was excited that his plan was back in action. He rubbed his hands together and smiled at Shaniqua. "We doing it, baby!"

Shaniqua smiled back, but it wasn't as wide of a grin as Reggie would have liked.

She must really be hungry, he thought. He remembered their earlier conversation.

"Don't worry, ma," he said. "We'll get to a restaurant and eat something as soon as this is over."

Shaniqua nodded, then went to go sit on a bale of hay.

Poor baby, Reggie thought. He would have to do something real nice for her later on. His eyes went back to Marlena, and for some reason, her presence irritated him.

"Yeah, I can't wait to get rid of this bitch. Gonna leave me for Junior like I wasn't shit. Now y'all can have each other forever." Reggie laughed in Marlena's face, and the confusion in her eyes mixed with fear only made him laugh harder.

He walked over and nudged Shaniqua. "She doesn't get it, baby. You see? She doesn't get it."

Shaniqua chuckled. "Right, she doesn't." Then she looked at the ground like she was sad.

Reggie turned back to Marlena, then looked down at Shaniqua once again. "Shaniqua, why don't you tell Marlena what her man did to get them both in trouble?"

***

As Shaniqua told the story with what Marlena knew to be fake excitement in her eyes and tone, Marlena became extremely pissed. She wished with all her heart that she was the one with the gun rather than Reggie. The reason he was planning to kill her and Junior was dumb as hell.

She wished her mouth wasn't taped so she could tell him so. He was gonna kill her, anyway, so why not cuss his ass out with her last words?

Marlena was mad at Junior for catfishing her, but at this point, none of that even mattered. Judging from the way Reggie was showing his true colors today, she was glad he had done it.

She couldn't believe she never saw signs that Reggie was crazy. Junior never mentioned it. Reggie never acted any type of way during the brief time Marlena dated him, and now, here she was, taped to a chair and facing the end of her life.

***

Reggie was pleased when Shaniqua finished the story. Marlena was looking at him like she wanted to tear him to pieces but wasn't shit she could do while duct taped to that chair. His heart panged for a second as he thought about what could have been.

Had Marlena not believed Junior's scheme, Reggie and Marlena might still be together. He wouldn't have had to do all he had done today.

This was all Marlena's fault.

Junior and Marlena. They deserved each other.

Reggie faced Shaniqua. "We gotta find a way to get Junior back here now so we can really get this party started."

Marlena started mumbling something through the duct tape that was over her mouth, but of course, no one understood what she was saying. Still, Reggie decided to fuck with her. He cupped his hand over his ear and leaned toward her. "I'm sorry? What were you saying? For some reason, I can't understand you."

Marlena struggled for a few more seconds, then she just gave up and glared at him from her seat.

Reggie couldn't wait to get started on her ass. He had a few tools in his trunk that were calling Marlena's name.

He pulled Shaniqua's phone out of his back pocket. He'd taken it back from her after she got off the phone with Marlena.

"Hey, you wanna see if we can..." he started, but they heard a car pulling up outside. Reggie shook his head. "This again?"

He went to look and saw that it was Junior. The frustration that was previously building within him turned to elation. Reggie grinned as Junior hopped out of his whip, coming straight for him like he meant business.

He quickly put his gun in the back of his waistband, welcoming the fight.

"Showtime, motherfucker!" he said, spreading his hands out, then squaring up as Junior entered the building.

Chapter 39

Junior entered the building ready for action. As soon as he saw Marlena taped to that chair, he felt like the biggest scum of the earth. *Don't worry baby, I gotchu,* he told her with his eyes.

The look she gave him was indiscernible, but he couldn't focus on that right now. Reggie was beckoning for him to fight.

Full of adrenaline, Junior rushed Reggie and actually landed his first punch. They'd shadow boxed plenty of times during their youth, and Reggie had won every single time. Junior wasn't much of a fighter, though he could hold his own. He could grapple, but he played it safe most of the time when dealing with other guys from their neighborhood and school. Most of them never messed with him, anyway, partially due to the fact that there were rumors about Reggie's bodies, along with the fact that Junior was tall, so they figured he could fight.

Reggie spat out blood after Junior's blow to his jaw landed. They circled each other. "Come on, pretty boy," Reggie taunted. "Let's show these ladies why you had me fight all your battles."

Junior was caught off guard, due to being pissed at Reggie's words, so Reggie's blow to his rib hit him. It hurt. Reggie's fists were built like fucking bricks.

Junior knew he couldn't take too many of those hits or he would fold like a piece of paper. He couldn't go down in front of his baby. It was stupid as hell, but in this moment, Junior cared more about his pride and ego at the prospect of losing this fight to Reggie than saving his and Marlena's lives.

Shaniqua was just standing there, watching the interaction with what looked like hope on her face.

Marlena was also eagerly watching from her chair.

Junior threw another punch, but Reggie easily blocked it and threw a left hook of his own, which Junior ducked and dodged.

Junior quickly lifted his jean legs as they continued to circle each other. He was gaining confidence. It could have been that Reggie was just fucking with him, missing a blow that at any other time he would have landed, but he couldn't dwell on that right now. This was life or death.

His mind focused back on Marlena, and back on saving her from Reggie.

***

This shit is about to be too easy, Reggie thought to himself as he fought back a laugh. Junior's ass could never fight for shit. Granted, he wasn't horrible, but he wasn't anything Reggie couldn't handle with his eyes closed, either.

Reggie let Junior land that sorry ass punch for Marlena's sake. Deep down inside, Reggie still didn't want to kill his boy. He was sorry things had to end this way.

Junior lashed out again, and Reggie was tired of this shit. He easily blocked the punch and landed one straight to Junior's nose, causing his head to snap back and Junior to fall to the ground.

"Damn, homie!" Reggie said. "You got knocked the fuck out!"

Reggie's joke must have reignited Junior's rage because the next thing he knew, Junior was on top of him, and he was on the ground, blocking a series of blows from Junior's fists. His punches were starting to hurt. *Damn, did this nigga get his weight up or something?* Reggie thought before he did a move he learned on the streets and swept Junior by using a circular motion with his legs. Junior fell to the side, using his arm to break his fall, and Reggie took that as an opportunity to stand.

He decided that he wasn't done with the fight yet. In a weird way, this was his last chance to bond with his boy. Their last time facing each other like this, except this time, it wasn't a play fight or shadow boxing match. This was to the death.

Reggie shook the flashbacks from his mind of he and Junior as kids, but not before Junior got him again. Reggie had to admit, his boy was showing heart.

He actually had to struggle as he punched Junior in his ribs repeatedly while Junior tried to wrestle him to the ground. He finally got Junior off of him with an uppercut to the throat. Junior backed up, clutching his neck at first, and Reggie took that as an opportunity to finish the fight. He began raining blows so fast and so heavy, Junior didn't know what to do. He folded easily.

Reggie was on top of him, holding Junior in a sleeper hold when Shaniqua jumped on his back to try to get him off of him. He easily flung her away, and when she came back, he let go of Junior for a millisecond to knock her out.

Too bad, he thought, not allowing himself to be hurt by Shaniqua's betrayal. *I thought the bitch was a rider. Can't dwell on it, though.*

Junior finally fell asleep, and Reggie ran to the back room to grab another chair.

Chapter 40

Reggie brought the chair to the main room and sat it behind Marlena so she and Junior would be back-to-back. He had to move quickly since Shaniqua was a snake, and Junior would wake up again any second. He would hate to have to kill any of them before it was time. He glanced at Shaniqua and saw her still out cold on the ground. *Good.*

Reggie worked quickly to tape Junior's wrists and ankles several times to get him subdued, then he lifted Junior's body and practically flung him into the chair behind Marlena. He forgot just that quickly that he was trying to get him tied down before he woke up. Junior started coming to, but Reggie was already wrapping the tape around his midsection, connecting him to Marlena.

"Come on man, you don't have to do this," Junior said, looking winded.

Reggie wondered why Junior wasn't trying to struggle or fight him off, then he reasoned that all those punches to his ribs must have taken his strength.

Too bad, Reggie thought. *I wouldn't have minded another round before I killed him.*

Reggie finished Junior's midsection and admired his handiwork.

Another flashback tried to rise to the surface of he and Junior playing cops and robbers when they were younger, but Reggie shook it off with force.

"No, this is YOUR FUCKING fault. YOUR fault."

Junior started pleading again. "Reggie, man, you don't have to..."

Reggie walked over and taped his mouth shut.

Then he felt alone. Like the lost little boy he'd always been. Reggie placed his hands by his ears to stop them from ringing. He couldn't have one of his attacks. Not right now. The attacks would come sometimes when he felt overwhelmed or when he was about to do something similar to what he was doing to his best friend right now. Ever since his father disappeared during his childhood and he was left with no one but a mother who hated him. He'd endured years of abuse at her hands, then she ended up dying in a freak accident at work.

He didn't cry at her funeral.

He just stared at her in the casket as if he was waiting for her to pop her head up and dare him to shed a tear. *I told you, I don't raise no pussies,* was one of her favorite sayings.

Reggie never told a soul about what he'd endured living with his mother, but he figured people should have known. His teachers should have guessed it. All those times he limped to school. All those times he found it hard to sit directly in his seat in class.

Then, when he stopped showing up on a consistent basis, they should have put two and two together. Reggie had nobody. Junior had a momma and a daddy.

Reggie didn't have shit.

Then, when Reggie got with Marlena, he had finally found a girl he really liked. Only for her to break up with him, then end up with Junior.

Hell no, he wouldn't feel sorry. Junior had made this bed. Now he had to lay in it. How dare he cross Reggie when Reggie had been nothing but loyal?

All those times Reggie held Junior down, and this was how he was repaid.

"Naw, fuck that nigga," Reggie said, more to himself than anyone else.

Junior was still mumbling through his tape, and so was Marlena, but none of that mattered. Nothing mattered anymore.

Reggie was on the dark side now.

Chapter 41

Shaniqua moaned as she came to, then she felt vomit rise to the top of her throat. She released her insides, or what was left of whatever she ate yesterday since she'd spent the entire day today in the abandoned building with Reggie.

The side of her head where Reggie hit her was pounding. She had no idea how Junior survived all of those punches.

She was still lying on the ground on her side, and a cramp was starting in her lower abdomen. She turned slightly as she moaned again, then opened her eyes to refocus.

She was staring down the barrel of Reggie's gun.

Shaniqua would have screamed, but she felt it was no use. No matter what she did, no matter how many plans she had made, they always seemed to fall flat. Now, the little inkling of hope she had previously was gone.

There was no way Reggie would believe she was on his side after she'd tried to defend Junior.

She opened her mouth to say something, but Reggie cut her off.

"It's showtime, baby girl. Get up."

Shaniqua allowed a tear to flow freely down her face as she got up, not even caring that she still had vomit on her left cheek. Reggie, however, wasn't having it.

He held the gun to her face with one hand and quickly wiped her vomit from her cheek with the thumb of his other hand, then licked it.

Shaniqua fought the urge to retch again. *Sick bastard.*

Reggie looked like he noticed her disgust. "What?" he grinned. "Tastes like chicken." Then his eyes darkened. "Come on. Let's go."

Shaniqua wordlessly followed Reggie out of the building while Junior and Marlena mumbled under their duct tape, trying some last-ditch efforts to get their attention. Once they were outside, Reggie locked the main door from the outside, then walked around to the side door to ensure that one was secure as well.

Shaniqua's heart sank. She was hoping somehow Junior and Marlena would escape while she and Reggie were outside. There was no way they could now since both doors had pretty sturdy outside locks, along with the additional security of chains.

Her tears flowed more freely now. "What are you going to do to them?"

Reggie turned to her, his expression indiscernible at first, then he looked irritated. "Stop all that damn crying! It's your fault I couldn't do my original plan for Marlena!"

Shaniqua didn't even want to know what Reggie's original plan for Marlena was, but still, she reduced her tears to a few sniffles.

She followed Reggie to the first of the three buildings without saying another word, then she asked again. "What are you gonna do to them?"

Reggie whistled as he opened the door to the first building, then ushered Shaniqua inside. The first building was set up similarly to the third one, except the furniture was different. There were a couple of tables, more bales of hay, then a random chest that looked like it was from the 1800's or something, that was laying on its side and wide open.

"How did you find these buildings?" Shaniqua asked. "How did you know you could use them for your plans?"

Finally, Reggie answered her, but he might as well have not responded. "That's neither here nor there," he said. "Besides, if I told you, I'd have to kill you. Just know that it's showtime. All this shit is about to be over."

***

Reggie was glad Shaniqua finally shut the fuck up. Her questions were more than irritating. They were weighing on his conscience like a motherfucker. That sad look in her eyes. The fear that shone through. He almost didn't want to kill her like he was about to do the others, but he had no choice.

None of them left him with a choice.

If Shaniqua held in her betrayal just a bit longer, she would have had him convinced.

Too bad, he thought. *I would have given her the world.*

Chapter 42

Junior's heart broke as he watched his oldest friend walk out of the abandoned building with full intentions on ending his life. He had no idea what Reggie planned, but it couldn't be good. There wasn't time to dwell on it, however. Even if it took all his strength, Junior was desperate to free himself and Marlena.

Junior prayed they would have more time together, that they would somehow survive this. There were so many things he wanted to say to her. He wanted to apologize. He wanted to let her know he never meant for any of this to happen. Both of their mouths were taped, so they couldn't say anything to each other.

But Junior still had his blade.

Miraculously, Reggie had missed it again, despite the fact that he put him in that sleeper hold and had ample opportunity to find it in his pocket. Junior hadn't even put it in his side pocket this time. It was in his main pocket where he would have easier access. All he had to do was get his hands over to his pocket to get it out, then he could begin the process of cutting the tape to free himself and his baby.

Junior twisted his arms at multiple angles, and he felt Marlena moving behind him, likely trying to free herself as well. Reggie had them both wrapped pretty tight, but if Junior could just reach the blade...

Perspiration was running down his forehead, and he had damn near dislocated his right shoulder, but Junior got his hands to his pocket where the blade was located. He twisted his fingers at an angle to reach the tip of his pocket as Marlena almost tipped their chairs behind him.

"Stop!" he mumbled through his tape, though he knew she wouldn't be able to understand him. He was trying to let her know that he had a way out.

Marlena seemed to get his message because she stopped moving. Once again, Junior twisted his fingers, his shoulder searing with pain. The blade was out of reach. He held his breath and twisted further. Still, out of reach.

Finally, he twisted again and quickly shifted his legs in a jumping fashion, and the tip of the blade stuck out of his jean pocket. Sweat clouded his vision, but he used his forefinger and middle finger to grab the tip of the blade, willing himself not to drop it by accident. His hands began cramping as he inched the blade out of his pocket, until finally, he got a good grasp. He flicked it open, then turned it so the sharp side faced the edge of the duct tape that held his hands together. He squeezed his knees together and rested the blade there, then quickly, but carefully began to move the tape up and down against the blade to rip it. After he got part way through, he went ahead and wrenched his hands apart with all his might, ripping the rest of the tape off.

Marlena began mumbling again behind him. He ripped the tape from his mouth.

"Baby, I got it!" he said, his voice choking up with emotion. "Hold on. I'm gonna cut the rest of the tape."

Now that Junior's hands were free, the rest was easy. He cut the tape from his midsection next, freeing his body from the chair, then cut his ankles free.

After that, he worked on Marlena, which was a much quicker job.

Marlena rose to her feet, and they faced each other, finally free. Now all they had left to do was get the hell out of this building. "Baby..." Junior said, and reached out to hug her, but before he realized what was happening, Marlena hauled off and smacked the shit out of him.

***

"How fucking dare you?" Marlena seethed. Abandoned damn building or not, Junior had a hell of a nerve, and a whole lot of explaining to do.

"Baby, wait..." he said, trying to stop Marlena's fists from getting to him.

"No, fuck you, Junior! You almost got us killed. You had to know Reggie's ass was crazy. You've been around him your whole life!"

Junior still had her arms subdued. "Listen, Mar. I'll explain everything, I promise, but now is not the time or place. We have to get the hell out of this building before Reggie comes back and shoots us, or whatever the hell else he might be planning."

Marlena snapped out of her rage. Junior was right.

They ran to the side door and tried it, but it was locked from the outside.

Marlena's heart sank before they even got to the main door and saw the same thing.

There were windows in the building, but they were so high, they needed something to stand on to reach them.

"Shit!" Junior said. He turned to Marlena. "Baby, we're going to get out of here. We just gotta find something to stack up to get out of the windows."

Marlena looked around, but all she saw was the two chairs they had been taped to, and a bunch of bales of hay.

She and Junior had the same thought, she could tell. They rushed toward the chairs first.

Chapter 43

Shaniqua felt so weak just standing there while Reggie paced back and forth, looking like his excitement was building. As he continued to pace, she was looking around the room for something that could be used as a weapon.

Unfortunately, just like with the other building, there wasn't shit. Just bales of hay, that big ass chest, and some tables. *Should I try to run?* she asked herself, but something told her that wouldn't work, just like her other plans hadn't worked. Reggie would likely shoot her dead, or even worse, chase her and catch her, then torture her until she begged for mercy. She shook herself out of those thoughts and focused once more on Reggie.

Reggie was talking to himself, which she hadn't noticed at first, but when he looked at her and saw that she noticed him talking to himself, he stopped.

"What are you going to do to Junior and Marlena?" Shaniqua asked. "Why did we come all the way to this building? I don't get it."

Reggie grinned and pulled out a remote-control looking device from his front pocket.

This nigga sure got a lot of shit in his pockets, Shaniqua mused.

"What's that?" she asked.

Reggie's smile widened. "It's gonna be epic."

"What's gonna be epic? What are you going to do?"

Reggie waited a beat, like he was contemplating whether he should tell Shaniqua his plans, then shrugged. "I'm gonna blow their asses to smithereens."

Shaniqua's jaw dropped. "What do you mean, blow them... you have a bomb?"

"BOOM!" Reggie shouted, scaring the living daylights out of Shaniqua due to the suddenness of the sound. "I'm about to fuck these niggas up. I've been dying to use this method of killing somebody. Guns and shit get boring after a while."

Shaniqua didn't know which question to ask first, but still, she asked the obvious. "You've killed people before?"

Reggie nodded, looking half filled with pride and half ashamed, then Shaniqua felt like an idiot. Of course, Reggie had killed people before! He just strangled Regina with his bare hands and shot Corey in the chest. How could she forget so quickly?

Shaniqua's mind was all over the place. This entire day was like a horrible nightmare that didn't ever seem like it was going to end.

Still, she had to do something. She couldn't let Reggie set off that bomb. In her heart, she knew she was going to die today, but with the shred of hope and dignity she had left, she wanted to try to save Junior and Marlena.

"Reggie," she started again. "Why a bomb? Why not just use one of your other methods? I mean, people are going to hear the explosion. Plus, your car is parked right behind their building. Not to mention, Junior and Marlena's cars out front. How are you going to get away?"

Reggie looked like he was unfazed by her line of questioning. "Don't worry about all that. Your betraying ass is gonna be dead, anyway. Why are you worried about me?"

Shaniqua's heart panged at those words. First, because Reggie looked like he genuinely had feelings for her, despite her supposed betrayal. Secondly, because she had liked him so much when she first met him that she felt she would do anything for him. She was living by attraction and emotions and look where it landed her.

"What are you planning to do to me?" Shaniqua asked.

Reggie ignored her question and continued the conversation about Junior and Marlena. "This bomb shit is about to be epic," he repeated. "Their bodies are gonna be unrecognizable. I built the shit myself. Junior's ass thought he was so smart all those years in high school. I fucked with math and science, too. Bet he never knew that. Bet his ass never figured that I could put something like this together. Everybody always said, 'Oh, Reggie's so dumb. Reggie's never gonna amount to anything.' Well, look where the hell Reggie is today. Fuck all y'all. Muthafuckas."

Shaniqua didn't know how to respond to what he'd just said because his eyes became vacant as he spoke, as if there was no light in him, and that Reggie wasn't there anymore.

He turned to her, and she had to look away.

"These motherfuckers aren't even gonna be eligible for a closed casket funeral. All they're gonna have are bits and pieces. Junior thought he was that nigga because he had his mom and dad growing up. How about now? When your momma and daddy won't even be able to identify you!"

Chapter 44

Junior worked with Marlena to pile bales of hay on top of the chairs so he could climb up and try to get out of the window first. They figured Junior would have an easier time since he was taller. He was praying this plan would work. Who knew where Reggie had gone with Shaniqua and when either of them were coming back?

Finally, all of the bales of hay were piled. Junior climbed up on top of the chairs first, then Marlena held the backs of the chairs while he tried to climb the hay. He got to the top, but he still wasn't tall enough. There was a wooden ledge running around the length of the building, so he climbed that, too, but there wasn't much support for his feet, due to the fact that it was so thin. Junior could reach out and touch the window now. He looked for a way to open it, but of course, there wasn't one. The windows were built into the building, and when Junior observed the glass, he saw that it was very thick. There was no way he would be able to break it without some kind of tool.

"Fuck!" he shouted.

"What is it?" Marlena said. "You can't open it?"

He didn't want to answer her question, but he knew he had to. This was no time for pride. He swallowed and looked back down at her. "No."

Then he looked back up at the window and punched it as hard as he could. Of course, that didn't do shit but hurt his hand. He punched it again and again, but absolutely no damage was done to the window.

There was no way out. He and Marlena were trapped in this building, and they were going to die.

Junior dropped back down from the ledge to the bales of hay, then went to the floor to stand with Marlena.

"We just gotta come up with another plan," she said, trying to encourage him.

"Ain't shit we can do, Marlena!" Junior blinked back his tears. He didn't want to snap at her, but at this point, he felt himself losing hope.

Marlena's lower lip trembled. "Junior, we have to at least try."

Those words renewed him. Junior ran into the main door with all his might to try to break through the wood. He figured since the buildings were so old, the wood might give. Unfortunately, as pain seared through his shoulders, it didn't.

Still, he tried again and again, until Marlena told him to stop. "Come on, you're gonna kill yourself trying it that way."

He turned toward her, full of agitation. "What the hell do you suggest?"

Marlena paused before she spoke. "Junior, this isn't the time to turn on each other." "Why the hell not?" Junior asked. "Didn't you turn on me when you sent Shaniqua to befriend me? You set me up, Marlena! Why the hell would you do that? You and Reggie."

Marlena held her hands up. "Wait, first of all, I had no idea Reggie was even in on this, and that was your fault that he was. If you hadn't catfished me and fucked up our relationship, I wouldn't be in this situation right now."

Junior was wounded by those words. "What are you saying? You're saying our relationship didn't mean anything to you? After three whole years? After I even got down on one knee and proposed to you?"

"Psshht, your proposal wasn't shit if you were carrying on a whole secret ass relationship with Shaniqua! I saw the damn screenshots, Junior!"

"What fucking screenshots, Marlena? I never did shit with Shaniqua. Granted, I should have told you about our friendship, but I never even looked at her that way. We were literally just friends."

Marlena shook her head. "I can't believe you."

Junior was pissed. "What is there not to believe? And what screenshots are you talking about? The only messages you would ever see between me and her is us talking shit back and forth about the arcade games. That's it. I told Shaniqua from the beginning that I had a girl, and she said she respected it."

Marlena looked confused, and Junior wondered why.

"What did your screenshots say, Marlena?" Junior wasn't the brightest bulb in the box, but he was starting to put two and two together. If he catfished Marlena using that Instagram model's photo and a fake profile he created, who's to say Shaniqua didn't do the same?"

Marlena was staring at him like she figured it out, too. Then, her expression darkened. "That doesn't mean shit. What were you doing going to her house at three o'clock in the morning? Why sneak out if you weren't planning to fuck her?"

Junior felt embarrassed for the answer he was about to give, but he figured he might as well tell the truth. "It was stupid, I know that now, but she said she needed help fixing her computer. I was already up, and you were knocked out... I don't know, Marlena. I was just trying to help a friend."

"You mean you were trying to help yourself to some pussy, or whatever the fuck she got down there!" Marlena spat.

Junior blinked. "What do you mean, whatever the fuck she got down there?"

Marlena didn't answer his question. "We gotta find another way out of this damn building." It wasn't her change in direction, it was more so the fact that she looked uneasy that made Junior even more curious.

"What did you mean by what you just said, Marlena?" he asked again.

She still didn't answer his question. Marlena pulled one of the chairs out from underneath the bales of hay, then tried to hurl it toward the window.

Of course, that didn't work. The chair didn't reach the window, it just hit the wall, then when it fell to the ground, one of the legs broke off. She picked up the leg, then tried to throw it at the window, too.

At this point, it was clear she was just stalling.

"Marlena, you know that shit ain't gonna work. Just tell me what it is."

Finally, she turned to him. "Shaniqua was born a male."

Junior's eyes widened, and he stepped back from Marlena. "And you tried to set me up to fuck her? What the hell is wrong with you?"

Marlena blinked back tears. "That's not all."

"What do you mean, that's not all?" Junior's mind was swimming. He couldn't believe that Marlena would do something like that to him. Yes, he'd cheated once before and, he hurt her, but she said she forgave him. She accepted his proposal a week ago. Junior thought he and Marlena were good. He'd never given her any indication he was attracted to the same sex or that he was curious about a transgender person. Why would she do something like this?

"Junior," Marlena said, snapping him out of his thoughts.

He faced her again.

"I'm sorry for setting you up. It was my fault you and Shaniqua became connected in the first place, despite the fact that I didn't know she was working with Reggie, too, but I do want you to know that I tried to go after you when you left. Corey..." Her voice broke. Junior understood why, because her cousin was dead, as was Regina. "Corey sent me a message right after you left."

"What did the message say?"

"I was trying to save you!" Marlena said.

Junior didn't respond, and she continued. "Corey said that Shaniqua had HIV."

Wow. Junior recoiled at those words. He had to put more physical distance between himself and Marlena now. It was one thing to try to embarrass him by having him unknowingly sleep with a transgendered person, but to try to infect him with HIV was a whole other level.

This was some sick shit. Half of him was happy all this had come to light. He could never marry a woman like Marlena now. Yeah, he had fucked up, but to try to kill him? This was crazy.

"Junior, I swear I had no idea! I promise you," Marlena said.

Junior didn't bother trying to decipher whether or not he believed her. He had to try to find a way out of this building. He walked away from Marlena without another word and went to the back room to check it once again.

Maybe he had overlooked it when he scoured the room the first time, but there had to be something there to help them get out.

Chapter 45

Marlena watched as Junior ransacked the back room like a madman. She knew he wouldn't find anything to help them get out. It was a lost cause. What bothered her more at the moment was the fact that it didn't seem like he believed her when she said she was trying to save him from getting HIV from Shaniqua.

"Junior," she said, trying to get his attention. He refused to look at her. "Junior," she repeated. "I swear, I would never try to set you up like that. Yes, I did some stupid shit with Shaniqua to see if you would go after her, but I did that shit because I had to know you would never cheat on me again. I accepted your proposal because I loved you, but when you cheated and got that girl pregnant, you broke me."

Marlena paused. She hadn't meant for that last part to come out that way, but it did.

Junior stopped his pointless endeavor and turned to her. "Marlena, I never meant to hurt you like that. I made a dumb decision. If I could turn back the hands of time, I would have never messed with that girl, but you gotta believe me, I had no intentions of cheating with Shaniqua. I wish I had my phone to show you our real conversations. Everything was platonic. I never kissed her, never flirted with her, hell, I never even held her hand. The only woman I had eyes for after you took me back was you. I would have never cheated in the first place if I had realized how much I loved you. You're the first woman I ever felt this way for. I was stupid, and I apologize. I acted like a little boy going after that girl to try to prove something to myself. I didn't prove shit, and I almost lost you as a result. Marlena, you gotta believe me."

He was begging her, just like he did that night she took him back in the pouring down rain. This time, however, Marlena had some pleading of her own to do.

"Junior, I believe you, but you have to believe me that I would never try to have you infected with HIV. I swear, when Corey sent that message, I went straight out the door after you."

They stared at each other, both of their breathing becoming more labored. The combination of the feelings from the dire situation they were in, along with the fact that they had just shared their deepest vulnerabilities about their relationship, coupled with a sense of renewed passion for each other as they saw one another with a new set of eyes, caused their next set of actions.

Before Marlena knew it, she was tearing at Junior's clothes, pissy jeans and all.

Junior was doing the same with her, grabbing her up in a passionate embrace.

They kissed like they never had before. It was passionate, it was potent, and it was heartfelt.

Even if they died tonight, they would die together, knowing they ended things with love.

***

It was time, Shaniqua knew it. Reggie kept mumbling something to himself over and over again. He had been slowly unraveling all day long, and now it seemed he was in rare form. She couldn't make out what he was saying, but it sounded like some kind of chant. Finally, he said something that sounded coherent.

"Momma didn't raise no pussies... no pussies... no pussies...." he kept whispering, over and over again.

"Reggie, what are you talking about?" Shaniqua asked, trying to break him out of his trance. It didn't work.

He kept chanting, over and over again, then, his voice grew a little louder. It was starting to scare Shaniqua, even more than she was already terrified.

"Reggie!" she said and grabbed his arm.

He snapped to attention, startling her.

For the first time, Shaniqua saw fear in Reggie's eyes. While he was doing his chanting, he had that faraway look, but the fear showed that he was still in there, somewhere.

"I'm really about to kill my day one over some bitch," he said.

"So don't do it," she urged. "Go ahead. Give me the remote." She held her hand out.

For a second, Reggie looked like a scared little boy. His hands trembled as he held out the remote. Shaniqua reached to grab it, but his eyes darkened again, and he snatched it from her grasp.

"Fuck that shit!" he growled in a vehement tone. "These fuckers gotta pay."

"Reggie," Shaniqua said, but she knew she lost him.

"Muthafuckas gotta pay," he said again, then he took a deep breath. "Here we go. Building 1A, say goodbye." He pressed a green button on the remote, then Shaniqua heard a beeping sound coming from the back room.

Reggie froze, then his head whipped toward her.

Shaniqua's heart dropped. "Reggie, did you say..."

Before another word could be uttered, the bomb went off.

Purely out of reflex, Shaniqua dove into the open chest that was laying on the ground, while Reggie spread out his arms and tilted his head back, embracing his doom.

Chaos ensued all around Shaniqua before everything went black.

Chapter 46

Junior had just finished making love to Marlena for what might be the last time. They lay in the afterglow for a few moments, staring into each other's eyes, then they got up and started putting back on their clothes.

"Want to give the main door another go?" Junior asked when they finished.

Marlena nodded.

Junior chuckled. "Maybe I can use my blade this time."

They walked out of the back room and toward the main door, but before they even got halfway there, an explosion sounded. They heard a loud boom from somewhere in the distance, then heard crashing and banging sounds. A large piece of one of the other buildings pierced through the window of their building, and Junior and Marlena were blown back from the impact of the main door and part of the wall of their building being penetrated by shards of glass and mangled wood from one of the other buildings.

Caught completely off guard from the blow, Junior and Marlena were both knocked out.

***

Marlena woke up in a daze. There was smoke all around her, and Junior was nowhere in sight. She saw

164

her car off to the distance with a large piece of glass going straight through the windshield.

She sat up, coughing.

"Junior?" she said, her voice barely above a whisper. "Junior!" she said a little louder. She heard a creaking sound and looked up. Above her, it looked like the ceiling of the abandoned building was about to cave in. She had to get the hell out of here.

She scrambled to her feet, trying to see through the smoke. She took a step to try to get to Junior, but her foot landed on something squishy.

She looked down, and it was a head.

A human head.

Reggie's head.

Marlena let out a bloodcurdling scream, then the ceiling creaked again. "Junior!" she shouted. "Junior!"

She heard moaning, then her eyes shot to Junior, who was stirring under a piece of wood. He had a gash on the side of his head, but thank God he was still alive.

Marlena dashed over to him. "Baby, we gotta get out of here. The ceiling is gonna cave!"

She moved the piece of wood, which wasn't that heavy, so Junior could get up, but it looked like his leg was injured.

He rose to his feet as part of the ceiling started coming down.

It was an awkward position, due to the difference in their heights, but Marlena slung one of Junior's arms over her shoulder and hauled ass as fast as she could, pulling him out of the building.

They got out before the rest of the ceiling crashed down.

Marlena could hear sirens in the distance. From the sounds of it, as well as the colors of the lights that were swiftly approaching, it was the police, firefighters, and ambulances.

"What the hell happened?" Junior asked, still in a daze.

Marlena's lip trembled as she looked up at him, letting go of his arm. Junior stood on his own now. "Reggie's dead!" she said, then began heaving as she relived the image of his head, and how it felt under her feet.

Marlena gagged, repeatedly, but nothing came out of her. She could only imagine what happened to Shaniqua.

***

Officer Brenham surveyed the scene with his partner and the other officers, searching for bodies. Junior and Marlena were taken to the hospital via ambulances, but before they were taken, they told him there were at least two bodies that were thrown in a hole by the male perp, and that the male perp was dead, possibly along with his accomplice.

Of course, Officer Brenham had to make sure, as well as check for more possible bodies. He and his crew searched through the aftermath of the explosion. There was broken wood and shards of glass everywhere.

"Shit!" he said when he found a human head. It was a male. From the demented, yet serene looking smile on his face, Officer Brenham knew this was the perp. "Sick bastard," he said, then gestured for one of the other officers to check it out.

"Damn," said the other officer, Stokely.

"We found the hole!" yelled officer Roberts.

Brenham and Stokely walked over. Brenham peered into the hole and saw two bodies, one male and one female.

Then he squinted. His eyes might be playing tricks on him, but did the male just move his leg?

"Oh shit!" he said, then looked at the expressions on Stokely and Robert's faces. They'd seen the same thing. "Call over the EMT's. He's still alive!"

Chapter 47

Junior and Marlena were rushed to the hospital via ambulance where their lungs were checked for smoke inhalation, and they were also thoroughly examined for other injuries as a result of the explosion. It turned out that Marlena was essentially unscathed, aside from the psychological scars she would have to work through.

Junior didn't suffer from smoke inhalation, but he did have a sprained leg as well as a few broken ribs. The doctor said he should heal relatively quickly, however.

Then, there were the countless questions from the detectives to try to figure out what the hell happened between them and Reggie that could have resulted in multiple dead bodies as well as a bomb going off. Junior and Marlena each had only pieces of the story, but the end result they agreed on was that Reggie must have accidentally blown up the wrong building in his haste to kill them.

Both of them felt like idiots explaining Reggie's reasoning, as well as their own, but they were just grateful to be alive.

"We do have some good news, Marlena," Officer Brenham said, smiling at her for the first time after several hours of questioning.

"What is it?" she asked, almost afraid to hear his answer, despite the fact that whatever he was about to say was supposed to be good news.

"Your cousin... Corey, was it?"

Her eyes clouded, and she nodded.

"He's still alive."

Both Junior and Marlena's jaws dropped.

"What?" Marlena said. "Reggie and Shaniqua told me that Corey was dead! They said Reggie shot him in the chest, then threw him in the hole with that Regina chick."

Marlena was still trying to figure out how Regina played a role in all of this. She barely remembered the girl, outside of the picture that ended she and Reggie's relationship years back. Junior and Reggie had mentioned her a few times, and when she saw her picture on Junior's social media a while back, she remembered that she had known Regina from high school, but other than that, she didn't know the girl.

Officer Brenham nodded, shaking Marlena from her thoughts. "Yes, Regina and Corey were thrown in the hole. Unfortunately, Regina did die as a result of Reggie's strangulation, but Corey is currently in ICU. The doctors are conducting an emergency surgery on him as we speak."

"My cousin is gonna make it?" Marlena asked, almost afraid to ask.

Officer Brenham smiled again. "We're hoping so. His situation is still very shaky but judging from the fact that he survived all those hours after being shot at such a close range, it's a definite possibility."

"What about Shaniqua?" Junior asked. "Did y'all find her?"

Officer Brenham's smile erased. "Yes, we did." He paused. "Unfortunately, Shaniqua didn't fare as well as Corey."

Marlena's eyes filled up again. "She died?" she swallowed. "She did try to save us."

Officer Brenham shook his head. "She's still alive, too, but she's hanging from a thread. One of the officers found her hanging from one of the trees in the woods behind the buildings. She must have been blown up there from the impact. Her body sustained a lot of trauma and she will likely never look or feel like herself again, but if she makes it through her surgeries, she's another miracle."

***

Junior and Marlena alerted their families to tell them about what happened to them as well as Corey, and all of their parents came rushing to the hospital.

They all sat in the waiting room for hours, praying that Corey would make it through his surgery.

Junior and Marlena each secretly prayed for Shaniqua, too. They knew she had helped cause all of the hurt and trauma they had faced, but they appreciated the fact that she tried to do the right thing in the end.

Chapter 48

Corey's eyes opened and the first thing he saw was a bright light. *Am I dead? Is this Heaven?* he thought, then he heard his cousin, Marlena's, voice.

"Corey?" she said.

Corey tried to turn his head toward her, but he felt weak as hell. He heard his mother's voice calling for the nurse, and a few moments later, the nurse came in. She asked him if he wanted her to raise his bed, and he agreed.

After about an hour, Corey was able to speak. His voice was scratchy, due to the tubes that were previously down his throat, but he was thankful to be able to see his family again. Especially his cousin, Marlena. He had so much to say to her, but he didn't know how to begin.

Corey listened as Marlena and Junior told him their parts of what happened that day with Reggie and Regina, then when they said Regina was dead, it broke his heart.

At first, his memory was a little fuzzy, but then he remembered why and how he ended up at that abandoned building in the first place. He was going there to try to fight some dude he thought Regina was cheating with, and now she was dead, and he'd almost lost his life in the process, too.

Marlena seemed to notice his change in demeanor. "What's up, Cousin? Why do you look so sad?"

Corey just shook his head. He wasn't ready to speak about Regina just yet.

***

Another week passed, and Corey was finally ready to speak. His voice was stronger, and due to physical therapy, he was feeling better. Marlena and Junior listened as he told them about how he had a secret relationship with Regina for months, and finally, Marlena and Junior seemed to understand how she fit into the story, though he wasn't fully aware what her part was himself, aside from what Regina had told him.

"Mar, I just pray you can forgive me for my behavior in this situation. I never meant to hurt you. I honestly thought Junior was cheating, based on those screenshots. I figured you would be better off without him."

He looked at Junior next. "I'm sorry, man."

Neither of them looked as if they held his actions against him.

Marlena spoke up. "Corey, you had no idea who Regina really was. I wish you would have told me about y'all secret relationship, but I understand why you did what you did. I'm still trying to figure out what the hell would make Regina lie to you about me like that? I barely knew the girl. I met her in high school, but she was only at our school for like a month." Marlena turned to Junior. "You knew Regina since childhood, just like Reggie. What the hell was up with her?"

Junior shrugged like he was stumped, too. "I mean, I honestly don't know. Regina was always cool, and she never gave me no bad vibes. We worked together and everything at the factory, all the way up until all this happened. I guess that's always gonna be a mystery."

***

Marlena finally found out the part Regina played when Officer Brenham informed her, Corey, and Junior about how they searched Regina's apartment that she shared with her mother and found a diary. Regina's diary had all kinds of crazy notes and pictures of both Reggie and Junior.

She also wrote a little about her part in the story. From that, the detectives were able to piece together that Regina was in love with Reggie, and that she hated Marlena out of jealousy and a weird obsession she had developed.

She contributed to what happened by playing Corey and making him feel like she cared about him, and plotting to help kidnap Junior, all as a result of a plan for revenge on Marlena for absolutely no rational reason.

"Regina's ass was just as crazy as Reggie!" Junior said when Officer Brenham finished sharing what his team found.

Marlena just shook her head.

Chapter 49

Two months later...

Shaniqua finally woke from her coma. When she did, at first, she was happy to be alive, but when she heard about the media frenzy that had ensued when the story broke about what happened, as well as the fact that she was facing such serious charges, she felt like she might be better off dead.

One of the nurses who worked with Shaniqua hated her, she could tell. She always looked at her with disgust, but Shaniqua didn't have the heart to ask for a replacement.

Instead, she allowed the nurse to talk nasty to her and treat her roughly when she was helping to manage her numerous injuries. Shaniqua's body was wracking with pain, day and night. She suffered from twenty-three broken bones, second and third degree burns on her face, arms, and legs, not to mention the psychological trauma of being held captive by a sociopath.

The doctors said it was a miracle she was alive, but Shaniqua felt more like a curse.

The doctors also said at first that she would likely not remember what had happened that night due to the severe physical trauma of the explosion, but that was a damn lie.

Shaniqua remembered every detail as if it was etched in her brain. At night, she was haunted by the look on

Reggie's face as he spread his arms to welcome his death while she dove into that chest, praying with all her heart that her life would be spared.

The doctors explained that the chest had saved her life by taking the brunt of the impact. It was pure speculation, since none of them were there, but they imagined that when Shaniqua dove into it and the explosion occurred, the chest must have closed up with her inside it, but then when the chest was thrown from the building, she was thrown from it and that was how she ended up in the tree.

Shaniqua didn't give a damn about their speculations. She lived a horrible existence in the aftermath of all that happened, and she had half a mind to ask Nurse Meanie to kill her in her sleep.

***

After another few days, Officer Brenham came to tell Shaniqua that she would soon face a court date and be transferred to a prison hospital. Shaniqua blinked back tears. "Will I be put in a prison with males or females?"

He stared at her for a second. "We'll advocate for a female prison."

By now, everyone knew she was transgender. Someone leaked that part of the story to the media, and that caused another uproar in the entangled tale of *A Love Triangle Gone Wrong*, as the story was being spun. It curled Shaniqua's stomach to hear about some of the things being said about her. Most of it was lies. Yes, she was a horrible person for what she had done, but she tried to right her wrongs. It was just too late.

Officer Brenham cleared his throat, shaking her from her thoughts. "Do you have any other questions?" he asked.

Shaniqua paused before responding. "Do you think I could speak to Junior and Marlena before I'm transferred?"

***

Nurse Meanie, as Shaniqua called her, entered her room almost immediately after Officer Brenham left her to her thoughts. Shaniqua wondered if the nurse had been waiting outside the door or something, listening in to their conversation.

The words that shot out of her mouth confirmed Shaniqua's suspicions. "You'll get what you really deserve in prison, you know," she taunted. "You'll rot in there, then burn in hell when you die like you deserve for what you did to that poor young couple."

"I'm already in hell now," Shaniqua said, sick of this lady's shit.

"Oh, no. You haven't seen anything, yet," the nurse continued. "Though God did give you a small punishment that you can take with you while you're here on Earth."

What is she talking about? Shaniqua thought, then she noticed the Cross necklace the nurse was wearing. Her lip curled up in disgust. Shaniqua had encountered malicious people all her life who claimed to believe in God. Thankfully, Shaniqua knew what real faith looked like through her mother's life. Shaniqua's mother had converted to Christianity shortly after she was diagnosed with cancer years ago, and she had lived a faith-filled life all the way to her death. This nurse was no Christian. Shaniqua refused to believe her words.

She opened her mouth to tell her so, but Nurse Meanie startled her by whipping something out of one of her large scrub pockets. It was a mirror.

Shaniqua looked at her reflection for the first time since her injuries, then she screamed at the top of her lungs until she passed out.

Chapter 50

Shaniqua had to go through her trial alone. Her family never gave a damn about her before all this happened, and the ones who held any sort of love for her previously had long abandoned her now.

She did get a chance to speak with Junior, Marlena, and even Corey before she had her court date and was transferred to a jail, thankfully. She explained her side of the story and apologized profusely, begging for each of their forgiveness.

They all said they forgave her but didn't want to speak to her anymore.

Once that happened, Shaniqua felt alone. She fantasized about ending her life, something she hadn't done since she was a child and used to cut herself. Nurse Meanie's words haunted her day and night, along with the memories of all that had happened. Thankfully, since she was set up in the jail's hospital, she didn't have much interaction with the other inmates. Only doctors and nurses, and the occasional inmate who came in for some kind of sickness or procedure. Shaniqua was grateful for that, and the fact that no one at this hospital messed with her like Nurse Meanie had. Her wounds were beginning to heal, but the pain in her heart felt like it would last forever.

The only person who seemed to be on her side was the prison chaplain, Reverend Samantha. Shaniqua was transferred to a female facility, as Officer Brenham had said, and the chaplain was also a female.

She didn't look at Shaniqua in disgust like most of the rest of society did. Instead, she sat with her for at least an hour every day. She prayed with her, allowed Shaniqua to open up about her childhood, and told her to trust in God.

Shaniqua was never sure whether she believed in God before all this happened, and she still wasn't quite sure what she believed about Him now.

She prayed and prayed every day, asking for forgiveness and another chance at life.

***

The day finally came for the verdict to be reached. To Shaniqua's surprise, Corey, Junior, and Marlena had all asked the judge to speak before the jury went in to make their decision. Each of them had advocated for her and asked for the judge and jury to be lenient, and reminded them that although Shaniqua had harmed them, she wasn't the true orchestrator of all that happened.

"If anyone deserved to go down for this, it was Reggie," Junior had said. "He was my best friend, but he told me repeatedly that day that he was the one behind all this. Shaniqua was just caught up."

"Shaniqua tried repeatedly to get Reggie to stop what he was doing, but he didn't listen," Marlena had said. "This is all on him, not her."

Corey couldn't speak much on Shaniqua's character since he didn't actually know her or interact with her, only Regina, but he tried to help, too.

The District Attorney was fuming in his seat, Shaniqua could tell.

She didn't know if her former friend's words would help her, but she was grateful they tried.

After two weeks of torture, the trial ended.

The verdict came in that Shaniqua was not guilty.

The jury was convinced that Reggie and Regina were the ones who were more culpable in everything that happened, based on all of the evidence as well as Corey, Junior, and Marlena's testimonies.

Shaniqua cried like a baby at her new chance in life. She didn't know where she would go from here, but she figured there was no way but up from rock bottom.

Epilogue

Two years later...

The time had flown by. Corey could not believe he had finally met the love of his life. At first, when he, Junior, and Marlena got out of the hospital, they underwent all kinds of interviews on both local and national news stations about what happened to them. They were offered both a movie and book deal after the first week.

Corey was against the idea, but Junior and Marlena were for it. He still felt guilty about the part he played in the saga, despite the fact that they forgave him, so he gave in.

The three survivors were the talk of the town, and they were seen as heroes. Shaniqua, unfortunately, was seen as a villain until the three banded together during a series of interviews to tell the real story of how Shaniqua factored into Reggie's plan. Once that happened, people started to back off, and someone even started a funding page for Shaniqua to get plastic surgery to help with her burns and disfigurement.

Corey was happy things were working out for his cousin, Junior, and Shaniqua, but he had to admit that his nights were still lonely.

He went to a counselor for months about Regina, as well as to try to figure out why the two women he had fallen for had both betrayed him in the worst way.

Through counseling, Corey was able to process his pain and build up his confidence. He grew wiser and more in tune to the traits people displayed, and he learned how to strike a healthy balance between wearing his heart on his sleeve and showing a woman he truly cared for her.

He didn't want to become some kind of heartless player, but he did want to be more assertive when it came to his love interests.

Finally, one day, he met his queen. Her name was Zena. He made a joke when they first talked about her being related to the warrior princess from the TV show, and Zena shared his sense of humor. They took things slow, dating and getting to know each other for six months before deciding to go ahead and become official. When they did, they met each other's families immediately, which was one of Corey's safeguards to know that he was dealing with the right woman. He knew he could be gullible and become blinded by his affections, but his cousin, Marlena, and his mom, Ivette, would be more likely to see through any bullshit.

Thankfully, Zena passed the test, and Corey passed through her family's scrutiny, too. Apparently, Zena had gone through her own share of failed relationships with men who played with her heart. When Zena's family met Corey, they instantly welcomed him, knowing he was a standup guy who would bend over backward for his woman.

He'd just proposed to Zena a week ago, and thankfully, she accepted.

He couldn't wait to embark on his new journey.

Corey straightened his tux in the mirror as he prepared to walk to the front of the church in a few moments and stand beside the pastor for Junior and Marlena's wedding. He was the best man, while ironically, Junior and Marlena had fully forgiven and invited Shaniqua to be the maid of honor.

Corey didn't agree with that idea at first, seeing that Shaniqua still did play a role in what happened to them on that fateful day, but apparently, Marlena and Shaniqua had rekindled their friendship. Since Junior was okay with it, Corey decided to leave it alone.

***

Shaniqua stood at the front of the church with the pastor feeling like a new woman. She winked at Trevor, her man, who was sitting a few rows back on her side of the pews. Trevor winked back.

She had met him when he performed a series of surgeries on her to help reconstruct her face. A funding page had been set up for Shaniqua after the media started to present her in a positive light. She'd had thousands of donors, who gave enough money to pay Dr. Trevor Hunt seven times over.

Nurse Meanie, otherwise known as Carolyn Jackson, had sent Trevor a long letter before he started Shaniqua's surgeries, basically begging him not to help her.

Trevor shared the letter with Shaniqua, and at first, she thought that he was going to tell her that she had to leave his office immediately. Instead, he ripped it to shreds, then informed her that he'd already sent a copy to her higher ups at the hospital she worked at. Carolyn was fired immediately.

Trevor and Shaniqua bonded during the long process of Shaniqua getting her physical appearance back in order, but after the surgeries were complete, they felt like their relationship had turned to something more.

Their first date, Shaniqua had spilled the beans about being transgender, though she was pretty sure Trevor already knew from the way her story had made headlines repeatedly.

Trevor, surprisingly, was cool with it, and their relationship went full force from there.

A few months later, however, before they were intimate for the first time, Trevor confessed to her that he had a secret of his own.

Before he even got the words out of his mouth, Shaniqua sensed what he was about to tell her. From his well-built physique, height, and full beard, most would never be able to tell, but Trevor, too, was part of the transgender community.

He and Shaniqua shared a laugh, then Shaniqua joked that fate must have brought them together.

A week later, Trevor proposed, and he and Shaniqua held a small ceremony to celebrate their union as husband and wife.

***

All eyes were on Marlena as she walked down the aisle to finally tie the knot with Junior, the love of her life. They had been through the storm and the rain, but after a five-year relationship, they were ready to make the leap.

Their original plan was to get married in a matter of months, but after what they went through with Reggie, both of them needed to heal. They went through relationship counseling, as well as individual therapy to push past their pains.

From both, they learned about themselves and each other, and they felt like all that they had learned had strengthened their bond.

Now, they were standing there, facing each other in a church filled with their family and friends. Neither had a shred of doubt in their minds that they were meant to be together.

The ceremony was beautiful, and there wasn't a dry eye in the room when Junior and Marlena recited the vows they'd created themselves, then shared a soulful, passionate kiss.

The reception was also a lot of fun with everybody dancing, eating, and having an overall good time.

Junior stared into Marlena's eyes as they danced the night away. "Damn, girl, you looking good." He cheesed.

Marlena's lashes fluttered. Junior's sexiness still made her heart skip a beat.

"Too bad this dress is going bye-bye as soon as we hit the hotel room," she said.

Junior's smile widened. "Shit, let's bounce right now."

***

When they reached their hotel room, just as Marlena said, it was on.

Junior took control, however. He wanted to pour all of his love into his woman tonight, to let her know again just how much he loved her.

He took his time, kissing and caressing her in all the right places. They started in the middle of their suite, then moved to the hot tub, then took a break and had a few drinks, then ended the night in their king-sized bed.

Their love was so full, it filled the room.

"Damn, Junior," Marlena said, breathless after their fourth round of lovemaking. "Marry me every day if that's how you gonna do it."

Junior smirked, then leaned over to kiss her lips again.

The End

Dear Reader,

I truly hope you enjoyed this story. If you did, please leave a rating or review to comment your thoughts on the book or characters.
Want to read another thriller? I have plenty more for you, all in different sub-genres.
Turn the page to explore.

Until next time,

Tanisha Stewart

The Maintenance Man: A Twisted Urban Love Triangle Thriller

"Momma said don't play with fire, 'cause one day, you might get burned..."

Malachi is a self-proclaimed ladies man; others would describe him as a dog. He sees women as disposable, despite the fact that he claims to be madly in love with his girlfriend, Zoe.

Everything appears to be going well for him, until the **bodies start dropping**.

Caught up in a race against time with too many suspects to figure out who's after him, it's time for Malachi to finally **come clean**. Is there a chance for Malachi's redemption?

Or is he just biding his time until his number is called?

Check it out here: <u>The Maintenance Man: A Twisted Urban Love Triangle Thriller</u>

Everybody Ain't Your Friend: An Urban Romance Thriller

They say you should keep your friends close, and enemies closer, but sometimes reality might be the other way around...

Mia thinks her life is completely normal. She has a loving boyfriend, great and supportive friends, and a close relationship with her mother.

Things take an interesting turn, however, when she is almost run down by a car one day. Then come the messages from an untraceable number. Not to mention the heartbreaking secret that is revealed shortly thereafter.

Suddenly, everything that Mia thought was right in her life goes wrong. She has no idea why, but she needs to find out, before her secret stalker decides her time is up.

Check it out here: Everybody Ain't Your Friend: An Urban Romance Thriller

Should Have Thought Twice: A Psychological Thriller

They say to always watch the quiet ones, because you never know when they might snap.

Shatina is a young woman with a troubled past and present. She lives in the shadows of her fraternal twin sister, who sucked up all the beauty genes, her best friend, whose seductive charm will sway any boy who listens, and her cousin, who is more than a knockout, but a force to be reckoned with.

Shatina feels like she has nothing going for her but her grades and her full scholarship to a four year institution of her choice... until someone comes along to threaten that.

Shatina has faced threats before, and little does anyone know, she has gained vindication over all of her enemies, one by one. Except this last one might be a bit more of a challenge than she bargained for.

Check it out here: Should Have Thought Twice: A Psychological Thriller

Not What It Seems: A Christian Romance Thriller

Girl meets boy. The feelings are mutual. It naturally follows that there will be a **happily ever after,** *right?* **Wrong.**

Priscilla is new to town, but she's not new to her faith in God. She visits a church she feels will meet her needs, and where she can serve. The only thing left is to make some friends, and she's good to go. She meets a group of Christians her age, which just so happens to include the sexiest man Priscilla has ever laid eyes on: Raheem.

Priscilla and Raheem's eyes meet when they are introduced, and the sparks fly immediately. One would think that the two are a match made in heaven, and that everything would move smoothly for them.

Wrong again.

Because now that Raheem has found someone he is serious about, strange things begin to happen that no one can explain.

Sinister things.

The new girl, Priscilla, may just become a casualty... But as the saying goes, *all's fair in love,* **and war.**

Check it out here: <u>Not What It Seems: A Christian Romance Thriller</u>

Caught Up With The 'Rona: An Urban Sci Fi Thriller

Cordell's luck could not be any worse. A young black man, a full-time student, doing his best to give back to his community by serving as a substitute teacher, only to receive an email which stated that his job would be suspended for the next three weeks due to the Coronavirus.

Frustrated about the situation, he vents to his lifelong friend, Jerone. Shortly after their conversation begins, they are approached by Markellis, a neighborhood hustler who always tries to sell Cordell and Jerone on his get-rich-quick schemes...

But this one is different. Cordell is pressed for cash, so he convinces Jerone to go along with Markellis' proposal.

No sooner than they say yes, Cordell and Jerone are swept up in an almost unspeakable conspiracy, with less than three weeks to turn it around...

Only it's much more than just Cordell and Jerone's lives that are at stake.

Check it out here: Caught Up With The 'Rona: An Urban Sci Fi Thriller

December 21st: An Urban Supernatural Suspense

Flick is a regular guy, living a regular life, then the night of Thanksgiving came.

It all started with a conversation he had with his cousin Bru that got a little heated.

Tensions rose, but things calmed down when he went to his mother's house for the family dinner.

Little did he know, that's when his life would begin to shift in a direction that he never expected.

December 21st, Saturn and Jupiter aligning, competing belief systems... what did it all mean?

Nothing, Flick thought.
Until the first event.
Then the second.

Follow Flick's journey in this Urban Supernatural Suspense as he tries to figure out exactly what's going on.

Is he losing his mind?

Or does everything that is happening have a deeper meaning?

Check it out here: December 21st: An Urban Supernatural Suspense

Tanisha Stewart's Books

Even Me Series
Even Me
Even Me, The Sequel
Even Me, Full Circle

When Things Go Series
When Things Go Left
When Things Get Real
When Things Go Right

For My Good Series
For My Good: The Prequel
For My Good: My Baby Daddy Ain't Ish
For My Good: I Waited, He Cheated
For My Good: Torn Between The Two
For My Good: You Broke My Trust
For My Good: Better or Worse
For My Good: Love and Respect
Rick and Sharmeka: A BWWM Romance

Betrayed Series
Betrayed By My So-Called Friend
Betrayed By My So-Called Friend, Part 2
Betrayed 3: Camaiyah's Redemption
Betrayed Series: Special Edition

Phate Series
Phate: An Enemies to Lovers Romance
Phate 2: An Enemies to Lovers Romance
Leisha & Manuel: Love After Pain

The Real Ones Series
Find You A Real One: A Friends to Lovers Romance
Find You A Real One 2: A Friends to Lovers Romance
Janie & E: Life Lessons

Standalones
A Husband, A Boyfriend, & a Side Dude
In Love With My Uber Driver
You Left Me At The Altar
Where. Is. Haseem?! A Romantic-Suspense Comedy
Caught Up With The 'Rona: An Urban Sci-Fi Thriller
#DOLO: An Awkward, Non-Romantic Journey Through Singlehood
December 21st: An Urban Supernatural Suspense
Should Have Thought Twice: A Psychological Thriller
Everybody Ain't Your Friend
The Maintenance Man
Not What It Seems

Made in the USA
Coppell, TX
17 November 2021

65934234R00115